# No Shortcut Home

A Novel

Slaton M. Smith

# NO SHORTCUT HOME

Slaton Smith

**BOOKS BY SLATON SMITH**
*Kill on Command*
*The Education of a Killer*
*Killing Ana Molotov*
*It's Called Vengeance*

# No Shortcut Home

Copyright © 2020 Slaton M. Smith

This book is a work of fiction. Names, characters, places and incidents either are products of the author's imagination or used fictitiously. Any resemblance to actual events or locales or persons, living or dead is entirely coincidental.

All Rights Reserved.

No part of the book may be reproduced, scanned or distributed in any printed or electronic form without permission. Please do not participate in or encourage piracy of copyrighted materials in violation of the author's rights.

## Primary Characters

SEAN GARRISON: Pittsburgh native. Unemployed advertising executive. Reluctant CIA asset. Occasionally filled with angst. One of two survivors of Robert Water's *Disposable Patriots* program and victim of extensive human experimentation. Father of Michelle Molotov Garrison.

ANA MOLOTOV: "Sandy." Former CIA operative. Assassin. Mother of Michelle Molotov Garrison. Daughter of Sergei Molotov.

NATALIA MOLOTOV: "Nat." Daughter of Mikhail Molotov. Niece of Sergei Molotov. Adopted daughter of Pavel Fetisov. Beautiful and dangerous. Madly in love with Sean.

SERGEI MOLOTOV: Soviet defector. Former Spetsnaz officer. CIA asset. Bicycle shop owner. Father of Ana Molotov. Grandfather of Michelle Garrison. Uncle of Natalia.

MIKHAIL MOLOTOV: Spetsnaz. *Deceased.* Killed in action – Afghanistan. Brother of Sergei. Father of Natalia.

PAVEL FETISOV: Former Spetsnaz. *Retired.* Served with Sergei in the Red Army. Communications and technology expert. Adopted father of Natalia Molotov. Successful Washington D.C. area dry cleaner.

MIKE RICHARDSON: 1st Special Forces Operational Detachment. *Retired.* Friend of Sean. United States House of Representatives, Idaho, Second District.

DAVID O'CONNOR: Director of the Central Intelligence Agency.

MARK PHILLIPS: CIA Analyst. Special projects lead for CIA Director O'Connor.

ROBERT WATERS: *Deceased.* Former head of *Disposable Patriots* program. Rogue CIA officer accused of running an off-book assassination program.

# 1
## Ollie's Boxing
## Los Angeles, California

Bummbada, Bummbada, Bummbada, Bummbada.

The rhythm of the speed bag was hypnotic. Not a good thing for Sean and his OCD. He had lost track of how long he'd been hitting the bag. His arms were burning, and his grey sweatshirt was soaked with sweat. Everything else just fell away from his consciousness when he gave into the OCD that had plagued him the last several years. His meds helped but he needed to remain focused to keep from slipping. Repetitive actions such as the speed bag or lifting weights were challenges for him. To complicate matters, he had an unnatural compulsion to always be moving. Always be pushing his body. The result of this messed up mental health cocktail was an extreme level of fitness. At 6'3" and 215 pounds Sean looked the part of a professional fighter. Although with the shaggy hair, stubble and tan, he looked more like a surfer. LA was looking good on Sean.

Sergei Molotov had suggested the gym to Sean. Sergei, a former Spetsnaz officer and a gifted boxer, had gotten Sean a membership, coveted in LA as the owner had closed the gym to new members. Several top boxing and ultimate fighting contenders trained there. The gym had two boxing rings and two octagons. The gym had an old school vibe despite being sparkling clean and the "it" place to work out. Sean kept a low profile, working out at odd hours. Sean didn't care for the manic macho personalities of the UFC guys in particular.

However, Sean being Sean, made a friend. Three times a week Sean worked out with Stu Hammersmith. Stu was an entertainment attorney and had been working out at Ollie's for nearly a year. He was fascinated by ultimate fighting. Sean repeatedly told him it was barbaric and to just focus on learning to box. At 5'8" and 140 pounds and in his mid-50's, Stu was in no way, shape or form cut out to be a UFC fighter. He was a little bit bald, barely had any athletic ability, but he had heart and Sean respected that. Stu persisted with the UFC thing despite the lack of physical gifts.

"Sean!" Stu shouted from behind Sean.

Sean, still in a trance, didn't hear him.

"SEAN!"

No response.

Stu gave Sean a little shove.

"WHAT?" Sean snapped. Stu jumped backwards. Sean quickly saw it was Stu. "Stu!, Sorry buddy. I didn't know it was you."

"That's ok, I'll make a note to not sneak up on you."

Sean sat down on the bench next to the speed bag and looked up at Stu.

"Something's different here," Sean said, looking Stu up and down. "Let me guess . . . . Facelift . . . . tummy tuck . . . ."

"You're really funny Sean. The reason I'm here is to work out to avoid those vanity procedures."

"Me too."

"Whatever Sean. You look like you've been boxing and lifting since birth."

Sean waved a glove at Stu. "You're nuts." Sean looked Stu up and down and pointed at the trunks. "It's got to be the shorts!"

"They are trunks, Sean. Trunks."

"Right."

"And just not any trunks." Stu ran his hands over the front of the purple trunks as he spoke.

"Oh yeah? Special?" Sean said, smiling and unwrapping his hands.

"They were worn by Manny." Stu put his hand on his hips smiling at Sean in his ill-fitting shorts.

Sean pulled the sweaty sweatshirt over his head and stuffed it in his bag.

"The taco truck guy?" Sean laughed, knowing exactly who Manny was.

"Pacquiao." Stu lightly smacked Sean across the head.

"That was my next guess. What did those set you back?" Sean asked, smiling at Stu and wiping his face off with a white towel.

"Not too much . . . ."

"Maybe I should ask Mary when you have me over for dinner."

"Ha! Let's keep this between us or there will be no more dinners."

Sean put the towel back in his bag. "So, what do you want to work on today?"

Stu turned around and pointed at the octagon. "I booked 30 minutes in there today. We can spar."

Sean shook his head. "Really? I thought you wanted me to work with you on the speed bag?" Sean stood and placed his hand on the speed bag. He dwarfed Stu.

"I promise not to hurt you," Stu said, goading Sean

Sean smiled at him and sat back down and pulled the wraps out of his bag, shaking his head. He looked up at Stu. "You have your wraps right?" Stu fumbled with his bag and pulled a new pair out with a smile.

Sean looked at them. "I suppose you need a hand?"

"Yeah, just this one last time." Stu handed Sean the wraps and stuck his right hand out.

"Just this one last time then." Sean repeated and laughed. "Will you watch this time?"

"Of course!"

Stu watched Sean carefully trying to read his expressions. He cleared his throat. "You know, Mary and I were thinking about asking her niece over when we have dinner next week."

Sean stopped wrapping and looked up at Stu making a face that Stu knew translated to a 'no'.

"No. I don't need to be fixed up."

"A nice Jewish girl would be great for you."

"The answer is no."

"She's really a beautiful girl. A Stanford law grad to boot."

Sean looked back at Stu. "I'm certain she is."

"Just drinks then?" Stu smiled nervously.

"No."

"Fine. I won't mention it again."

"Good."

Sean helped Stu with his gloves and then wrapped his own hands for the second time. He slipped on a pair of punch mitts, removed his shoes and socks and followed Stu to the Octagon.

Ollie, a squat man with cauliflower ears, clad in grey sweats shouted to Stu. "Stu! You only have 25 minutes now. Diaz has this reserved for the rest of the afternoon."

"Thanks Ollie!" Stu said bouncing on his toes in the middle of the octagon.

Ollie looked at Sean. "Sergei is in town, right?" Sean nodded. "He said he'd stop in." Sean was hoping to avoid seeing him however. He was not certain where his relationship stood with Sergei and had no idea what his daughter Ana thought of him now. Sean still had trouble trusting either one of them.

Sean had on a loose black t-shirt and his nearly worn out WVU lacrosse shorts. He dropped his gloves by the side of the octagon. He watched Stu bouncing around. He circled Stu and telegraphed a jab that Stu avoided.

"I think I'm getting faster!" Stu shouted at Sean.

"Definitely!" Sean assured Stu. Sean held the punch mitts out to his side. Stu pounded away. He tried a couple of roundhouse kicks that Sean sidestepped.

"Good thing those didn't connect! You'd be out!" Stu stammered, out of breath.

"Nearly had me!" Sean bounced around a few times, allowing Stu to keep landing punches.

Stu stopped and put his hand up. "I need a minute." He put his hands on his knees. "You get your gloves on. We only have a couple minutes left. I'll let you get a few punches in."

"Sure thing." Sean dropped the punch mitts and walked over to the edge of the octagon to put on his gloves. Gathering around the Octagon were Carlos Diaz and his entourage. They were laughing at Stu. Sean stared at them as he put on his gloves. Diaz noticed.

Diaz hit the cage with his gloves. "What are you eyeballing, pussy!"

Sean glared at him but didn't respond. Diaz's entourage laughed and heckled Stu and now Sean. Sean walked back to middle of the Octagon.

"Stu, let's go."

Stu looked back at Diaz and his crew. "Nonsense! We have 10 minutes left. We will be here for 10 minutes."

Sean shook his head and took a couple of jabs at Stu, clearly distracted by Diaz who continued to shout obscenities.

"You know, we just hired a new receptionist at the firm. She's a Ms. California runner-up." Stu said smiling.

"Do I look that pathetic?" Sean asked, as he was jabbing.

"Well, yes."

Sean saw movement out of the corner of his eye. It was Diaz, striding towards them.
He had decided that Stu and Sean's time was up.

"Time for you queers to get out!" Diaz sized up Sean as he ordered them to leave. To Diaz, he looked like a surfer that was out of his element.

"You'll need to wait." Stu responded.

Diaz was about 5'11" and covered in tattoos. His trunks were black with orange yellow flames rising from the bottom of the garment. "Diaz" was written in script and was smack in the middle of the waistband. He was a few pounds lighter than Sean with little to no body fat. Carlos Diaz was a bad man. Sean recognized that the bulk of the tats were gang related, but he didn't think much more about it. Diaz was the #1 light heavyweight contender for the UFC title. Diaz's crew cheered him on from outside the octagon. A woman who appeared to be in her mid-20s was standing with her arms crossed behind Diaz's rabid crew. She was telling Diaz to stop and just wait. She was very attractive.
However, it was clear she was not his girlfriend.

Diaz extended his arm to push Stu. Sean's gloved hand shot out and deflected Diaz's jab.

"Ooooooo!" Was the reaction from Diaz's crew.

Diaz spun and stared down Sean, getting right up in his face. Sean's demeanor had changed in a split second – Stu saw it. Stu recognized that this had now escalated to a level he knew was heading to a bad situation. He removed the punch mitts and took a handful of the back of Sean's shirt to pull him away. Sean took a step back. Diaz laughed.

"Yeah! Better do what your sugar daddy says!" Diaz shouted.

Sean's anger boiled over. He placed his right gloved hand on Diaz's face and pushed him backwards. Diaz staggered backwards, both shocked and embarrassed that Sean would dare touch him.

"Did you just fuckin' touch me?" Diaz screamed, as a crowd gathered around the octagon.

Sean stood his ground and stared at Diaz. He slightly turned his head, eyes on Diaz. "Stu, get out of here."

Stu slowly shook his head, shocked at how the situation had gotten out of control. "Sean, let's go!"

"I'm going to fuckin' beat your ass!" Diaz screamed at Sean. The people that were watching, cheered and continued to heckle Sean.

"Stu, get out." Sean repeated. Stu picked up the mitts and left the octagon.

Sean gestured at the young Hispanic woman yelling at Diaz to stop. She was dressed in jeans and a red Holister t-shirt. She was pretty and looked like she had class – clearly no one Sean thought Diaz would date. "That your sister? I think I'll show her a good time after this. What do you think?"

Sean guessed right, it pissed Diaz off. Diaz began pumping his fists and came at Sean. Diaz was fast but Sean avoided his jabs. Sean didn't want to give Diaz the chance to get him on the canvas where he might have an advantage. On his feet, Sean would be hard to beat.

"You should have let us finish and kept your mouth shut." Sean taunted.

"Kick his ass!!!!" Diaz's crew screamed.

Sean took a few steps towards Diaz and connected with a series of jabs that snapped Diaz's head back. Diaz became crazed. He came at Sean with several wild swings. One connected with Sean's ribs, but was harmless. He grabbed and ripped Sean's t-shirt trying to pull him to the ground. Sean slipped away and bounced on his toes, smiling at Diaz

"I thought you were good." Sean mocked Diaz. Sean reached up and pulled off the torn shirt, revealing his collection of scars, including the gunshot wound to his shoulder. Stu was behind him outside the cage.

"Sean this is stupid. Get out of there!" Stu said.

Sean ignored him. He wanted this. He didn't know why. He just did.

Diaz's manager arrived and was telling Diaz to get out of the cage. After watching Sean move, the manager immediately knew Sean was not a random guy that worked out in the gym. He had a good idea where the scars littering Sean's chest came from and knew they were not from a car wreck. The manager was now worried about his fighter.

"Carlos! Get out of there. You're not a street fighter! You're training for a championship!"

Sean laughed at Diaz. "Better listen." Sean blew a kiss at Diaz.

Diaz charged at Sean with a flurry of punches. None hurt Sean. Sean then landed a series of jabs and a round house that stunned Diaz.

The manager took notice. "Stop this!"

Diaz waved him off and tried to set up Sean for a roundhouse kick. He went up in the air and spun to deliver the blow. Sean saw it coming, ducked and swept Diaz's leg sending him to the canvas with a painful thud. Sean was back on his feet bouncing on his toes.

Diaz wiped some blood from his nose and circled Sean.

Sean taunted him by tapping his elbows, telegraphing his next attack.

From the back of the gym, Sean heard a familiar voice. It was Sergei shouting in Russian, "Sean! No!"

In the same instant, Diaz swung at Sean. Sean deflected the swing and sent a crushing blow with his right elbow into Diaz's face that lifted him off his feet and onto his back. His nose was broken, and blood was flowing freely from his nose.

The gym was silent. Sean stood over Diaz, removed his gloves and let them drop to the canvas.

Two men ran into the octagon to tend to Diaz, followed by a disapproving Sergei.

In Russian, Sergei tore into Sean, "What were you thinking?!! You could have killed him!"

Sean left the cage. Diaz's crew got out of his way. He walked towards his bag, Sergei bending his ear every step of the way. Stu was there holding his bag. He was speechless. He looked up at Sergei, trying to figure out who he was. Sergei was in his 60's but didn't look it. His hair was blonde and closely cropped. His features were chiseled. Stu noticed Sergei's hands when he placed them on Sean's arm. They were huge, strong and menacing. Stu had never seen hands like that and never wanted to see them again. He swallowed hard and stood where he was.

Sean looked down at Sergei's hand on his arm and then back up at Sergei. "Get you hand off of me." Sean calmly warned.

Sergei ignored him and continued in Russian, "Ollie is going to kick you out of here!"

Sean snapped back, "It's just a gym! Lighten up!"

Sergei got nose to nose with Sean. "You have to get this under control."

Sean took the bag from Stu and began taking off his wraps. Stu stared at the scars on Sean's chest and shoulder, curious about their origin. Part of him didn't want to know.

"Thank you." Sean took the sweaty sweatshirt out of the bag, pulled it over his head and stuffed the wraps in his bag.

"I'm leaving. You can keep yelling at me in the parking lot." Sean said and started to leave.

"Sean. Are you ok? What was that?" Stu asked, stunned that his seemingly harmless friend had just bested one the best MMA fighters in the country.

Sean turned. "I don't like bullies."

# No Shortcut Home

Stu watched Sean leave the gym with a large Russian on his heels yelling at him.

## 2
## Ollie's Gym
## Los Angeles, California

Sean burst out of the gym and into the midday sun with Sergei right behind him. He threw his bag over his shoulder and briskly walked towards his bike wanting Sergei to just disappear. Traffic flew by in both directions in front of the gym. A group of people were on the sidewalk waiting for the bus. Sean didn't want to hear a lecture. He also thought the trip to LA to see Ollie was Sergei's lame excuse to talk with him about Ana.

Sean was respectful of Ana and kind to her, but Ana wanted to be more than a friend and was in love with Sean. Sean still could not trust her, or Sergei for that matter. The fact that Ana was the mother of his daughter was the only thing keeping him in California. He loved his daughter Michelle more than anything and wanted to be near her. Ana knew that and based on her prior behavior, Sean thought she was using the baby to try to rekindle something with him.

"Sean! You can't do that kind of thing!" Sergei lectured.

Sean spun around and faced Sergei. "What? What can't I do? That guy came into the octagon and began to shove my friend, so I stepped in. Did you see that part?"

Sergei paused. "No, I didn't, but I saw you finish it. You should have walked away."

Both men stood in the middle of the parking lot. Sean didn't answer.

"Sean, please be careful. You need to keep a low profile for many reasons. And, whether you like it or not, we care about you." Sergei tried to smile, patted Sean on shoulder, looked in his eyes, turned and got into his truck.

Sean stood where he was. Now, he also felt like shit. Sergei didn't look back. He pulled out of the lot and drove away.

"Damn it!" Sean mumbled. He walked over to his bike and pulled his helmet out of the bag. He began to start the bike, but stopped. He put both hands on the bars and stared down at the bike's tank. While Diaz deserved a beating, Sean realized he shouldn't have jumped at getting into a fight.

Josie Diaz came out of the gym, clearly disgusted with her brother. She briefly glanced at Sean slumped over his bike but didn't give it a second thought. She headed for a little white Mercedes.

A beat up grey mini-van roared into the parking lot. Sean looked up as it flew past him. The van skidded to a stop next to the Mercedes. Josie hurried to get into the car. Three men, covered in tattoos, dressed in jeans and white t-shirts jumped out of the van. Josie slammed her door shut. One of the men began banging on the top of the

Mercedes, screaming at Josie. Another was looking at the door of the gym and telling the other two to hurry. The third man grabbed a baseball bat out of the van and smashed Josie's driver's side window, sending glass all over her and the parking lot. Both men began fighting with her and pulled her out of the car.

Sean was already off his bike with his helmet in his hand. The lookout saw Sean rapidly approaching and was screaming at him in Spanish to stop or they'd kill him. Sean kept moving forward. The man began to reach behind his back for what Sean thought was a gun. Sean swung his motorcycle helmet and connected with the side of the man's head, sending him to the parking lot pavement in a heap. The other two noticed Sean. One grabbed Josie by the hair and slammed her face into the side of the van. She fell to the ground.

"You're in the wrong place, dude! This is none of your business!" One yelled at Sean and raced towards him with the bat in his hands. He took a big swing at Sean. Sean deflected it with the helmet, stepped to the side and delivered a kick to the man's knee. There was an audible snap and the man fell to the ground, yelling at Sean and clutching his knee.

The last man, stepped over the unconscious Josie, reached into the van and pulled out a shotgun. Sean was now moving fast. Before the man could turn with the shotgun, Sean threw his helmet, connecting with his head. It didn't knock the man down but gave Sean the instant he needed to cover the ground between them.  Sean grabbed the shotgun with both hands.  Sean and the attacker were face to face.  The man stared back at Sean with pure hatred.

"She's my property!" he screamed, spitting in Sean's face as the words flew out of his mouth.

 Sean found leverage and punched the barrel into his face, causing him to release the shotgun.  He fell into the open door of the van.  Sean cleared the weapon, flipped it in his hands, grabbing the end of the barrel with both hands and bringing it crashing down on the man's head as he jumped out of the van at Sean.  He hit the side of the Mercedes and then the pavement.   Sean threw the shotgun into the Mercedes.  He kneeled down and checked on Josie.  She was moaning and blood was dripping from her nose. Sean scooped her up in his arms and hustled her towards the gym.

Two men exiting the gym held the door open.  Sean rushed into the gym with Josie.  Ollie saw Sean first and rushed from behind his desk.

"What happened!"

"She was attacked in the parking lot.  Three guys."

Sean kept moving through the lobby and into the gym. Ollie was right behind him.

Carlos Diaz was in the octagon sparing and was the first to see his sister in Sean's arms.

"WHAT THE FUCK??!!!" Diaz pulled his gloves off and ran out of the octagon.

Ollie directed Sean to a training table and he gently placed Josie down. As soon as he placed her on the table, he was tackled by two of Diaz's crew. They knocked Sean to the gym floor and began to rain blows down on him.

"I was helping her!!" Sean shouted. They didn't care or didn't hear. Ollie tried to pull them off with no success. They began kicking Sean in the ribs. Sean covered his face to protect himself.

"STOP! STOP!" Josie shouted at them. When they heard her voice, they stopped beating on Sean. He lay on the floor with the men standing around him, now looking at Josie. Carlos was standing by the table trying to look at her face. She pushed him away.

"He saved me. If he had not been there – I'd be gone." Josie's voice quivered as she spoke.

Carlos leaned over and whispered into her ear. Josie nodded at her brother. Carlos kneeled down next to Sean, patted him on the chest. He stuck out his hand and helped Sean to his feet.

"Thank you." Carlos stuck his hand out. Sean shook it. Carlos looked over at his crew. There was a collective "sorry."

# No Shortcut Home

Ollie threw Sean a towel. He patted his nose and wiped the blood off of his face. Sean put his hand on Josie's back.

"You OK?"

She tried to smile at Sean, "I'm OK. Thank you."

"You're welcome."

Sean headed for the door. The gym watched him. Carlos caught him before he got to the door.

"It's Sean right?"

"Yeah." Sean turned. Carlos' attitude had changed completely.

"Thank you."

"You're welcome." Sean turned to leave. Carlos grabbed his arm.

"She's paying the price for my mistakes."

Sean looked at the tattoos and got it. He was certain that Carlos' gang ties were the reason. Carlos noticed Sean's glance at his tattoos.

"I'm out. I quit." Carlos said, answering an obvious question.

"Good."

"They're making it hard."

Sean ignored the response. He was tired and really didn't want to engage. He clearly had misread Carlos and was feeling especially shitty for pounding on him earlier in the day.

"Take care of her." Sean opened the door to leave.

"You back in tomorrow?" Carlos asked.

"I think I need a day off."

Sean walked out of the gym. The three men and their beat-up van were gone. His helmet was nowhere to be seen.

"Damn it," Sean mumbled under his breath. Could be worse he figured. Sean got on his bike and left.

## 3
## Sean's Apartment

Sean rode into the garage under his building and parked his Ducati next to his Jeep. After all, he couldn't go everywhere on the bike as much as he wanted to, and the Jeep was a pretty cool alternative. He got off the bike, tightened the bag that was thrown over his shoulder and walked to the staircase that opened to the building's courtyard.

Sean figured the building was constructed in the 1950's. There were two floors, all with outside entrances. The building was a perfect square and each apartment overlooked the courtyard. It was not big or fancy, but the landlord had taken tremendous pride in the property. The landscape was mature, and everything was a shade of green that Sean found calming. The pool was small but always clean and there was a community grill that Sean used nearly every night. The landlord was an ex-Marine in his late 60's who screened everyone with incredible diligence.

Sean crossed the courtyard, waved to a couple of people and climbed a second set of stairs and walked a few dozen feet to his apartment. He opened the door, walked in and placed his bag and keys on a table near the door. Sean's place was essentially one room. The small kitchen was separated from the living space by a peninsula bar. Near the door was a picture window. Under the window, Sean had added a club chair and ottoman. A queen size bed was between the door and the kitchen. Opposite the bed was dresser. A stack of a dozen or more books were stacked on the dresser. There wasn't a TV in the room. Sean thought about getting an old set but it was hard to find one and he gave up. There was no way in hell he was putting a "smart" TV in his place – too easy to hack. On the kitchen bar was an off-yellow phone – a land line. Sean hadn't had an iPhone or cell phone in two years. When he needed to make a cellular call, he bought a burner, used it and tossed it after one use. A door led to a modest bathroom and closet. On a table next to the bed was a picture of his daughter, Michelle.

Sean crossed the room, sat on the edge of the bed and picked up the picture of Michelle. He stared at it for a long time. Ana had never stopped him from seeing her and he visited as much as he wanted, but Ana was always there. Sean knew Ana loved him, but he still could not trust her. He felt Ana was using the baby to pull him in. When people met Ana, they thought Sean was nut for not putting a ring on her finger.

What they didn't know was that Sean met Ana through work. Ana's job was to kill the freshly - programmed Sean if he got out of line. She was to drop him with a shot to the head if he deviated from any instruction. Ana then manipulated Sean to extricate herself from the influence of a nasty, rogue CIA agent, after which she tossed him aside like yesterday's news. At least that's how Sean saw it. Now she wanted to get back together and pretend everything was normal. Kind of hard to trust someone after that. Plus, no aspect of Sean's life could any longer be considered normal.

Oh, and then there's the fact that Sean fell for and ran off with Ana's cousin Natalia, who for all intents and purposes dumped him. Sean had not heard from her in months. He woke up one morning and she was gone. Sean tried to contact her every couple of weeks, but never had any luck. Sergei believed she was with the Mossad. Sean had no idea, as she was illusive when it came to talking about herself. She had one thing going for her that Ana didn't. She'd never used him or set him up to be killed. That was a big check in the "pros" column.

Sean put the picture back in its spot on the table and walked into the bathroom, pulling his shirt off as he walked. He passed the mirror and stopped. His ribs were beginning to turn black and blue. He wasn't sure if it was Diaz punching him or his crew kicking him. Either way, he was sore. He was lucky one of the kicks didn't break a rib or catch him in the face or head. He turned on the water for the shower.

Sean dressed and pulled a couple of hamburger patties and three beers out of the refrigerator. He placed them in a small insulated bag along with some cheese, buns, a plate and spatula. On his way out of the apartment, Sean picked up a book off the top of stack, left the apartment and went out to the courtyard. He found a spot at a table near the grill. He sat down and took a beer out of the bag. He leaned back in the chair and took a sip, watching people in the complex come and go. Most waved at him.

Eventually, Sean got up and cooked his dinner. He sipped on a second beer and took his time eating. The apartment was in the middle of Los Angeles, but the courtyard felt like an oasis. Sean couldn't believe he found it. The best part was that no one knew where he was. As far as Sergei and Ana knew, he lived in an extended stay hotel on the other side of town. While Sean was patting himself on the back, an older woman approached him.

"Good evening, Mrs. Lomax." Sean said standing as she came to the table. She was holding a plate of cookies. "Would you like to sit down?" Sean pulled out a chair for her. Mrs. Lomax was in her early 70's, always smiled and was generally a happy person. Her hair was grey which was a contrast to her dark complexion. She typically dressed in tan capri pants and a golf shirt. She also had an obsession with expensive running shoes. Today, she was wearing a hot pink pair of Nikes. Her husband was the first African-American television producer in Los Angeles. He produced the top morning show in LA for years.

"I'd love to Sean. Thank you." She placed the plate on the table. "I baked these for you today."

"Wow! Are these chocolate chip?" Sean answered, picking one up at the same time.

"They are. I know you love them." Mrs. Lomax was thrilled to have someone to bake for. Her husband was diabetic and was not supposed to be eating the wonderful stuff his wife baked.

"I do!" Sean smiled and pulled the last beer out of his bag.

Sean looked at her feet. "New pair? They're sharp."

Mrs. Lomax extended her leg. "Yes, they arrived today." She looked around. "Don't let Mr. Lomax know."

"Your secret is safe with me." Sean replied and laughed. "As long as you keep the cookies coming."

"That's a fair price for your silence!"

They both laughed and Sean reached for another cookie and then remembered his manners.

"Mrs. Lomax, do want a beer? Sorry I didn't offer earlier."

She laughed out loud. "Thank you, Sean, but I have not had a beer in 20 years!" She kept laughing. "But, thank you!"

"You're welcome." Sean put a second cookie in his mouth.

Mrs. Lomax leaned back in the chair, clearly wanted the distraction that Sean provided.

"So, Sean how are things down at the shelter?"

Sean nearly choked on his beer. "I was off today. I went to the library. I worked out. That's it. Nothing exciting."

When Sean first met Mr. and Mrs. Lomax, they had asked him what he did for a living. Sean couldn't say "nothing". Of course, "nothing" is better than "I kill people." He didn't want them thinking he was a deadbeat so he blurted out the first thing he could think of which was "I work for the animal shelter." Mrs. Lomax thought it was the greatest thing she had ever heard. Mr. Lomax asked "How do you make any money?" Mrs. Lomax smacked his arm before Sean had to make up another lame lie.

"Not exciting! Sean, you're living an exciting life and I love hearing about it."

Sean knew she genuinely loved talking to him.

"You're too kind Mrs. Lomax." He smiled big.

"I also like that you're always reading. However, Mr. Lomax thinks it's weird that you don't have a TV."

"He seems to like it when I come by and watch the Dodger's games with him."

"He loves that. He also likes teasing you."

"I can tell."

Mrs. Lomax got up from the table. Sean rose from his chair. "There are more cookies upstairs. You're always welcome to come by."

"Thank you."

Sean smiled. He liked living here.

# 4
## Ollie's Gym
## Next Morning

Sean sat on the bench next to the speed bag unwrapping his hands. Turned out he was not expelled from the gym. He was breathing heavily and had sweated through his navy sweatshirt. From across the gym, Carlos Diaz was walking towards him. Sean continued with his wraps.

Diaz stopped a few feet in front of him. Diaz was getting ready to train and was wearing old grey sweats. They looked to be older than Diaz.

"It's Sean right?"

Sean remained seated and unwrapped his left hand. He looked up at Diaz. "Yeah."

Diaz rocked back and forth, clearly uncomfortable. "Thank you again for helping both of us yesterday."

"How did I help you?" Sean asked with a bit of a tone, stuffing the wraps in his bag and looking back up at Diaz.

"My sister told me I needed a taste of humility and you delivered it. Believe it or not, you've given me the push I need before the fight."

"Glad I could help." Sean said sarcastically. He picked up his bag and placed it on the bench. He hoped Diaz was leaving but he wasn't.

# No Shortcut Home

"I'd die if something happened to Josie. She's the one in the family that is going to do great things."

"You seem to be doing ok." Sean responded.

"No. It's her. She's smart and she's driven. Yesterday is why I paid for her to attend the University of Michigan. I want to get her out of here."

"That's a great school." Sean answered and began to understand and respect Carlos Diaz.

"She was the first person in our family to graduate from high school and then she graduated from Michigan. We are so proud of her." Diaz said, getting emotional.

"That is great." Sean wished he had something better to say than "great" but couldn't find the words.

"Now, she's in law school."

"Really? Good for her."

"Yes, in Michigan. I use whatever money I make to pay for her school and for my mother's house. I want them away from the life that took my father and my brothers."

Sean now saw Diaz in a new light. Yesterday's events now were much clearer.

"That's very generous."

"I want something better for both of them."

Sean still couldn't resist a jab at him. Verbally. "You know, you're a bit of a dumbass."

"What??!!" Diaz said, instantly angry.

"The short, bald guy you were yelling at yesterday is a partner in the largest entertainment law firm in LA."

Diaz kneeled down and cupped his head in his hands. After a moment, he looked at Sean and stood back up.

"You're shitting me."

"I'm not."

"I guess I fucked up Josie's chances there."

Sean stood up and threw his backpack over his shoulder. "Maybe not. I'll see what I can do."

Diaz slapped Sean on the shoulder. "Thank you!"

Sean turned to go.

"One more thing."

"What's that?" Sean asked, turning around. He was going to be late for his job at the animal shelter.

"My mother heard what happened and wants to have you over Saturday for dinner."

Sean thought for a moment. "Sounds good. Thank you for the invite."

"She'll be really happy. So will Josie. I'll text you the address. What's your cell?" Diaz asked, fishing his iPhone out of his pocket.

"I don't have one."

"What? You don't have one? That's fuckin' weird, dude." Diaz had a puzzled look on his face.

"Just tell me the address."

Diaz told Sean the address and time.

Sean winked at him and pointed at his head with his index finger. "Got it. See you Saturday."

"Oh, we only speak Spanish at home. Just letting you know."

"No problem," Sean answered, smiling.

"You're fuckin' strange, man."

"Yeah, I've heard that from time to time."

Sean left the gym and headed to the animal shelter for his six-hour shift.

# 5
## Province Khuzestan, Iran
## Saturday - 9AM – Local time

Colonel Farshid Shirazi had worked his way up to the top of Iran's Islamic Revolutionary Guard Corps (IRGC). He now handled all intelligence operations in the region and around the world. He had the ear of Iran's prime minister and the trust of the Ayatollah. No small feat, making him one of the most powerful men in Iran.

Shirazi took a sip of his coffee and looked out at the barren landscape. The Chinese were in to talk about upping the shipments of Iranian crude. He saw the United States' sanctions on Iranian oil as illegal. The Chinese thought the sanctions were a joke and never had a second thought when they defied the U.S. The new U.S. President, Wilber Robertson had declared that the IRGC was a terrorist organization. Shirazi thought it both disgusting and hypocritical.

A staff member reminded Shirazi that the meeting was about to commence. He gathered several papers, placed them in a folder and walked down a long hall to the conference room. As he entered, his staff got to their feet as did two men from the Iranian Oil Ministry. Three Chinese men stood as well. They were clearly government bureaucrats. Shirazi greeted everyone, took a deep breath and a seat at the head of the table. The Chinese contingent took out files and placed them on the table, pulled out what looked like a purchase order and slid it to a member of the Iranian Oil Ministry. The man studied the document.

Shirazi knew Iran needed the funds, but also knew China was screwing them on the price. This stuff also bored him out of his mind. The Prime Minister had requested he attend to signal to the Chinese that Iran respected and valued the partnership. He got up from the table and walked to the window. He placed a hand on the window and watched people come and go from a building across the street. Out of the corner of his eye, he caught a flash in the western sky.

A second later, a GPS-guided GBU-38 precision bomb dropped from a MQ-9 Reaper flattening the building killing everyone inside.

# 6
# Fox Hollow Gun Club
## Friday – 9:30PM – Harrisburg, PA

President Wilber Robertson took a look at himself in the mirror in the private locker room of his favorite club. He owned 17 multi-million-dollar private gun clubs around the U.S. but had refused to divest himself in his interest in the clubs as well as his considerable oil holdings. Robertson's father had made billions in the oil business decades ago. His son simply collected checks. A shameless self-promoter, he was clever enough to parlay his wealth and notoriety into the highest office in the land. Since the election, the NRA and backers had poured millions into the clubs. Congress was screaming about it, but Robertson ignored them.

"Damn, you're beautiful!" the President mumbled to himself. Robertson was 6 feet tall but required his press office to list him as 6'3". The press office made certain that anyone standing next to the President was shorter to further the illusion.

His valet stood off to the side, always knowing what to say. "No woman can resist you. It's really not fair sir," he said.

"Right as always, Roger," the President responded while working on his chestnut hair. The President's daily routine took most of an hour. Image was everything. His hair had to be perfect as did his tan.

There was knock at the door. The President's chief of staff, Sloan Bennett, popped his head in. "Mr. President, we're ready for you down the hall."

"Tell them to wait!" He snapped, suddenly distracted by a television playing Fox News in the corner. He walked over to see if they were talking about him. There is nothing more important than television. After a few minutes, he turned.

"Time to go. They'll be talking about me in about 15 minutes."

Roger opened the door. Outside were two dozen people from the White House and Secret Service and another 20 club members lining the long oak paneled hallway. Sloan Bennett was next to the President as they walked down the hall. The club members applauded, and President Roberson seemed to bask in it.

"These people really should not be here, Mr. President." Bennett said.

"I say who can be here and who can't. Not you!" He snapped.

"Yes, Mr. President."

Several feet from the door, there were four men in their mid to late 50's dressed in hunting apparel and clapping. Bennett knew who they were and didn't like them.

"Did you get him?" One shouted as the President entered the conference room.

Bennett's head snapped around and looked at the man. The comment made his heart jump into his throat. The operation they just conducted was known by only a handful of people. He paused briefly and looked at the man who was wearing a smug look on his face. When he saw the Chief of Staff, the man made a "shooing" or "run along now" gesture.

Bennett was too busy to get pissed off, but he made a mental note. The cronies needed to be dealt with.

The heavy doors closed behind him and he got to work.

## 7
## Fox Hollow Gun Club
### Friday – 9:40PM – Harrisburg, PA

The President walked to the front of the room and took a seat at the head of the table.

"Well?" He asked impatiently.

General Stan McGimsey stood. "Mr. President, if you'll turn your attention to the screen, you'll see the building containing Colonel Farshid Shirazi and his staff."

Projected on the screen was a remarkably clear video of a building. Seconds later it was flattened.

The President leaned forward in his chair and clapped loudly after the explosion. The rest of the room was silent.

"Good work General. Good work!" The President shouted.

"Thank you, Sir. If I may continue?"

The President half waved at him.

"Three nearby buildings were damaged in the blast. The casualties are unknown. However, we 100% certain that Shirazi was killed in the blast."

The President looked around the room. "Where's O'Connor? I'd like to hear his assessment of my successful decision."

Bennett cleared his throat. "Sir, if you remember, you demanded that he be excluded after he argued that we didn't have clear proof that Shirazi was planning an attack."

The President's emotions were like a rollercoaster on some days. This moment was no exception. "That bastard! He needs to go! That's a topic I want addressed!" The President blurted out. Everyone in the room had known CIA Director O'Connor for years. The President continued, "Doesn't he remember that I declared Shirazi a terrorist??!!"

"I don't think he disagrees that Shirazi is a dangerous man. His second point was that Shirazi is a member of a sovereign state, which changes the equation," Bennett explained.

"I don't care what he said."

"Yes sir."

The room was silent.

"Is there anything else???!" The President snapped.

Bennett shuffled some papers and handed a statement to the President. He pretended to read it. "Sir, this is the statement the Pentagon will make at 10PM eastern time."

"Good." The President looked around. "You may leave."

Everyone began to gather their papers and headed out. The Chief of Staff got up from the table.

"You stay here." The President ordered. Two of the President's special advisors remained seated.

"Yes, Mr. President." Bennett answered, taking his seat.

"I want the three of you to find some dirt to give me ammunition to get rid of O'Connor over at the CIA."

"Mr. President, O'Connor is one of our brightest. I don't recommend it," Bennett argued.

The President screamed and slammed his fists on the table. "I don't give a shit what you recommend! He is not loyal to me and needs to go!" The President's face was red.

Bennett swallowed hard.

One of the advisors blurted out, "He's old. He's a dinosaur. Plus, you don't need a reason. You're the most powerful man in the world."

The President smiled.

The second man added, "The angle is we need new thinking for the new threats we face."

"I like it." The President answered.

"I can get a list of qualified replacements to you by the morning, sir," Bennett answered.

"I don't need a list. I have the perfect person."

"Who?"

"Peter Collins."

"The former mayor of Lexington, Kentucky?" Bennett asked.

"Yes. Is there a problem with that?"

"I don't see how his qualifications are adequate. In addition, I don't think we can get him confirmed. There's also a cloud of corruption surrounding him."

"Well, it's your job to solve it. If you don't, I'll find someone that will."

The President stood, followed by the two advisors.

"Oh, and Bennett fire that asshole by the end of the week."

"Yes, Mr. President."

"Last thing, tease this win in Iran with the press. After the Pentagon briefing, they will want a statement. Make them wait. I'll do something during primetime Saturday night."

"Yes, Mr. President."

The President left the room and Sloan Bennett slumped down in his chair.

## 8
## Fox Hollow Gun Club
## Friday – 10:30PM Eastern

Sloan Bennett exited the conference room and slowly walked down the hall. He could hear the President's booming voice and the laughter of his cronies. He pushed open the door to the men's room and shuffled past other members of the staff who were oblivious to the fact that the President essentially committed an act of war without even so much as an email to Congress. President Robertson believed that the president had complete control of all matters related to war and that over the last 25 years, Congress had ceded more and more power to the Presidency, making his unilateral decision OK.

Sloan Bennett looked at himself in the mirror. His suit was still blue and his shirt still white. His hair was a little grayer but the passion for the job had left his body.

He pulled his phone out of his pocket and dialed.

"This is David." CIA Director O'Connor answered.

"David, it's Sloan. We need to talk."

"I think we do. There's a Denny's off of Union Gap Road. Meet me there in 45 minutes."

"You're in Harrisburg?" The Chief of Staff asked, partially surprised.

"I figured you'd want to talk."

## No Shortcut Home

"See you there."

Bennett put the phone back in his pocket and splashed some water on his face.

# 9
# Denny's – Harrisburg
# Friday – 11:30PM

Sloan Bennett entered the Denny's, spoke briefly to the hostess and found the CIA Director in a booth in the back along with another man that he didn't recognize. The CIA Director was in his mid-60's, dressed in a navy suit. He was a little over-weight but not by much. What was distinguishing was his shock of white hair.

"Hello Sloan." O'Connor said as the Chief of Staff approached. "Have a seat."

"Thanks for meeting me." Bennett answered, looking at the other man at the table. "Who is he?"

"This is Mark. He's an analyst." Mark Phillips had been with the agency after he left the Navy and for the last 5 years had been working closely with the CIA Director. No one really knew who he was, which he was thankful for. He had on a red, quarter zip sweater, glasses and jeans. Unremarkable in every way.

"He have a last name?"

"No." The CIA Director answered. "Can you please hand him your cell phones?"

"Why?" Sloan handed two iPhones over to Mark Phillips. He then placed them both in an insulated bag. The Chief of Staff watched him with skepticism. "Is this really necessary?"

"Yes. I'm sure you're aware that the video camera and microphone on these phones can be activated at any time."

"Fine. I really don't care." Bennett answered, running his hand through his hair.

"You should. The Iranians have the capability to listen into any phone on the planet, including the unsecured iPhone your boss insists on using." O'Connor added.

"Fine. I don't want to relive that topic." Sloan Bennett snapped back.

"So, the President has begun an illegal war? Is that the most efficient way to put it, Sloan?"

"That's accurate. No meaningful notification of Congress. Of course, we have a large group of sycophants in both houses that will cover for the President."

"Anything else?" The CIA Director asked, knowing what was coming next.

"He wants you fired by the end of the week." Bennett looked at O'Connor for an outraged look of some sort. He didn't get one. Both the director and his analyst were stone faced.

"Sloan, that's not a surprise. I appreciate you speaking with me."

"You're welcome and I'm sorry." Sloan Bennett looked around the Denny's, like someone was listening to him. They weren't. The CIA Director had made certain of it.

"The President has larger problems however. The United States is vulnerable to a cyberattack that will paralyze the country."

"While the President never reads the briefing book, I do. How real is this?"

The CIA Director adjusted his glasses. "Oh, I'm afraid it's very real and it's coming." O'Connor looked over at Mark Phillips. "Mark?"

Mark Phillips pulled out a tablet and swung the screen around towards the Chief of Staff.

"For years, Iran has invested in cyber-warfare planning. They put their best and brightest in the program. In addition, they contract out to troll farms and hackers around the world. They are beyond clever, well-funded and next to impossible to track and locate." Mark explained.

"I understand that. So what?"

"Here's the so what. They have the ability to disrupt all air traffic, our power grids, our transportation systems and corrupt all of the cellular towers across the US. And there's more."

Sloan Bennett was leaning forward. "And?"

Mark pointed to a chart on his tablet. "This estimates that 61% of Americans will run out of food and water in 8 days if Iran launches a cyberattack. 80% of cars on the road will be out of gas in 4.3 days. The result will be riots. Most people only have enough food on hand for 4 days. In addition, they can send every train delivering coal, gas, chemicals and hazardous waste flying off the tracks all across the country."

"But will they do it?" Sloan asked skeptically.

"Oh yes." Phillips answered. "And they are going to."

"I'm going to guess that the President wants to address the country Sunday night." O'Connor said.

"Good guess." Sloan answered.

"It won't take place. Iran will have already begun the attack."

"WHAT?!!" Sloan screamed. The cooks in the Denny's kitchen stared through the kitchen's pass-through at the Chief of Staff.

"What are we doing about it?"

"Mark is working with the NSA. We're trying to locate where they are conducting the attack."

Sloan interrupted O'Connor. "Find it and we will blow the shit out of it!"

O'Connor waved his hand. "You sound like your boss. There's more to it." O'Connor looked to Phillips. "Mark?"

Mark flipped to a diagram. "Sending a rocket in to blow everyone to pieces will not do any good. These people are all working as part of a huge network. If you blow up one group, the rest of them will continue attacking us and probably ramp up the intensity."

"So, what do we do?"

"We find one cell, infiltrate it and install a virus into their system that will disable their systems and give us a backdoor that we can then use a for a counter attack. We'll also be able to locate anyone who logs into their network."

"Have we located one of their cells?" Sloan asked anxiously.

"No." O'Connor answered

"What the fuck have you guys been doing?" Sloan shouted.

O'Connor calmly took a sip of his coffee and stared at the Chief of Staff.

"David, I'm sorry. This job is going to kill me and I'm on edge. I didn't mean that. I know how hard you guys work and the sacrifices you make."

Mark cleared his throat. "The good and the bad. When the cells are not operating, they are planning and it's hard to track them. However, when they launch an attack, there's going to be a small window when it becomes easier to track them."

"An attack has to happen for us to find them? Great. Not the solution I wanted."

"It's the reality," O'Connor answered.

"And you're certain this is coming?" Sloan asked.

"My sources say the green light has been given. I also think you'll wake up tomorrow morning to millions of Iranians in the street of Teheran and nearly every country in the world condemning the President's actions. Oh, and the calls from Congress. . . . However, the phones may or may not be working." O'Connor predicted.

Sloan Bennett stared blankly at the Denny's placemat in front of him. "This is awful."

"I agree. We're working on a solution but it's going to get worse before it gets better." O'Connor added.

Bennett got up and reached across the table and shook David O'Connor's hand. "I'll try to talk President Robertson out of firing you. It's a bad decision."

"Thank you, Sloan, but don't risk your career for me. I'll be alright."

"Thank you, David." Sloan Bennett left the Denny's.

O'Connor looked at Mark Phillips. "Find Sean for me."

"I'm not sure where he is. He's becoming harder and harder to find."

"In about 14 hours, it's going to be next to impossible to find him when we lose every cell phone in the U.S. and the internet fails at the same time. Do it now." O'Connor ordered.

"I'll find him."

## 10
## Dinner with Mrs. Diaz
## Saturday - 4PM Pacific Time
## Los Angeles

Sean looked at the directions he had scribbled on a piece of paper. He pulled his Jeep over and studied the street signs. He missed the GPS on his iPhone, but there was no way in hell he was getting one now. Yes, Sean was paranoid and based on his recent past, it was for good reason. He turned right and slowly drove down the street. Up ahead he could see a row of cars and people walking up to a house. He guessed this was the place. Sean parked a few doors away and walked down the sidewalk towards Mrs. Diaz's house. The neighborhood was a quiet tree lined street populated with well-maintained mid-century modern homes. Sean had put on an ironed pair of khakis and a blue button-down shirt. He really didn't know what to wear. He had picked up a bottle of Patrón and a large bouquet of flowers for Mrs. Diaz. He figured he couldn't go wrong with flowers.

Sean rang the bell and looked around, listening to people talking and laughing inside. He heard the rattling of the door lock. Carlos opened the door and held his arms out with a big smile.

"Sean! Thank you for coming!" He hugged Sean and pulled him inside. This was a Carlos Diaz that he was not expecting.

Sean held up the bottle of Patrón. "I brought this for . . . ." Carlos took the bottle before Sean could finish his sentence.

In Spanish, Carlos shouted, "Everyone! This is Sean! He came with a gift!" The people in the living room all hooted and clapped.

He whispered to Sean, "I don't drink, but that's ok. Who are the flowers for?"

"I got them for your mother." Sean said in Spanish.

Carlos slapped him on the back. "Your Spanish is good! She's going to love you. Let's go see her." Carlos led Sean towards the kitchen. Sean nodded at Josie as he walked through the living room.

"Mama, this is Sean." Carlos said. Mrs. Diaz put down the dishes she was carrying, wiped her hands and smiled. Mrs. Diaz was barely 5' tall and looked to be in her 60's. Her hair had streaks of grey in it. Josie followed Sean and Carlos into the kitchen.

"Sean! Sean! Thank you for being here! I have been so excited to meet you!" She hugged him.

Sean was overwhelmed by the welcome. He held the flowers out in front of him. "I brought these for you." Mrs. Diaz put both hands on her face. Sean was a bit self-conscious about his Spanish but plowed ahead anyway.

"They are beautiful! So beautiful! Let me put these in water." Mrs. Diaz said, clutching the flowers.

## No Shortcut Home

She glanced at Josie. "Josie, get me a vase." Josie immediately scrambled for a vase. It was clear that when Mrs. Diaz told you to do something, you did it immediately.

"You're welcome and thank you for having me here." Sean said thrilled that $25 worth of flowers could make someone so happy. A woman passing by Sean in the kitchen handed Sean a beer and kept walking. Sean thought this couldn't be better.

"I love them! I just love them!" she exclaimed, arranging them in the vase.

Josie took out her phone, "Sean let me get a picture with you and Mama."

"Sure thing." Sean walked over and put his arm around Mrs. Diaz.

"Make sure you get the flowers in the picture, Josie."

"I did Mama."

Mrs. Diaz looked at flowers and then at Sean. "Josie, this is the type of man you need. And he's so tall!"

"Mama, please!" Josie pleaded.

"Thank you again, Mrs. Diaz." Sean added, not really knowing how to end this conversation.

"Sean, you make yourself at home. If you need anything, you come see me." Mrs. Diaz added, reaching up and patting him on the cheek. She went back to work in the kitchen.

Carlos slapped Sean on the back and led him out to the back yard. "Told you she was going to love you. I think she might adopt you."

"She's amazing. Thank you for the invite." Sean looked around the yard. Most of the people were from the gym. They recognized Sean and came up and shook his hand. One apologized for kicking him. Sean told him not to worry about it.

"Dude, what's with that accent?" Carlos asked, squinting at Sean.

"What accent?"

"Your Spanish is surprisingly good, but you've got a bit of an accent. It's weird, I can't place it."

Sean took a sip of beer, working on an excuse. "I picked it up in Spain."

"Spain?"

"Yeah."

"Ok. I don't give a shit. Just sounded strange."

"Sean, make yourself at home. I'll check on you later." Carlos walked back into the house.

## No Shortcut Home

The house had an outdoor kitchen with a firepit, sink and refrigerator. Mounted to the house was a modest sized TV. A baseball game was playing and along the bottom of the screen a "breaking news" crawler relayed news of the attack on Colonel Farshid Shirazi. Sean stared at the TV for a moment and then turned to go back in the house.

Josie stopped him in the living room. "Boy, my mother loves you!"

"She's great," Sean said taking a sip of his beer.

"Also, I wanted to say thank you. I thought they would leave us alone, but they just won't." She said, referring to the gang that was harassing her family. Josie was a little taller than her mother with long dark hair. She was wearing jeans and a red top. She smiled at Sean when she spoke.

"Glad I was there and I'm sorry this is happening to you."

"Where did you learn to fight like that? You destroyed Carlos and nobody destroys Carlos," Josie said, wanting to change the subject.

"I was just lucky. He'd beat me 9 times out of 10."

"It didn't look like luck."

Now Sean wanted to change the subject. "Josie, I almost forgot. Carlos said you're in law school."

"I am."

Sean reached into his pocket and fished out a business card. "You remember the guy I was sparing with?"

"Yeah, the guy my dumbass brother bullied?"

"That's the guy." Sean flipped the card between his fingers. "Anyway, he's a partner in the largest law firm in LA. Here's his card. He said he'd love to talk with you and to call next week."

Sean handed Josie the card. She just stared at it.

"Why did you do that?" She asked.

Sean shrugged. "I want you to be successful."

"You don't know me," she answered, holding the card in the palm of her hand.

"I think I do."

A tear ran down her cheek. She started to get excited. "Oh my god! Oh my god!" She startled Sean. He jumped a little. She turned and ran into the kitchen.

"MAMA! MAMA!"

Sean could see Carlos running in from the backyard. Sean got nervous. Front his vantage point in the living room, he could see Josie explain it to her mother and brother while jumping up and down. He could see Mrs. Diaz burst into tears and then walking towards him. She had her arms out to hug him. Sean hugged her back and she pulled him down to kiss his cheek. Carlos hugged him. The room was silent. Carlos clapped his hands.

"This guy just got my baby sister an interview with the biggest law firm in LA!" He slapped Sean on the back. Sean was certain he'd have a bruise on his back from Carlos slapping him constantly.

Sean had no idea they would react this way and was a little stunned. Suddenly, everyone in the room was shaking his hand and another woman placed a cold beer in his hand. He was really beginning to like it here. Sean had a third beer and munched on the food that was placed around the house. He'd been there for roughly and hour when he heard the kitchen phone ring. Josie answered it.

"Hello?"

"Hello. My name is David O'Connor and I'm calling for Sean."

Josie was a little puzzled. Why did he have calls forwarded here? How did he know the number? Was he a doctor? Her mother would really love that she thought.

"Sean?"

"Yes, Sean. He's about 6'3". Dark hair. Nice guy," O'Connor answered politely.

"One moment please." Josie walked out of the kitchen and into the living room. She tapped Sean on the shoulder, and he leaned down.

"Sean, there's a phone call for you in the kitchen."

Sean made a face. "Really? No one knows I'm here."

"A man named David O'Connor."

Sean went white and stood up straight. He could feel the color drain from his face. Josie noticed.

"Sean, are you ok?" She touched his arm as she spoke. "I can tell him you're not here and I made a mistake."

Sean looked over at the TV in the room and the crawler with news in Iran. "No, I'll speak with him." Sean walked into the kitchen and picked up the phone.

"Hello?" Sean looked around the kitchen while he spoke as if there was a camera on him.

"Sean, it's David."

"How did you find me?" Sean put his beer down.

"It turned out to be easy when we really drilled down. And if I remember, you were supposed to check in with me."

"I forgot." Sean answered.

# No Shortcut Home

"Hmmm." O'Connor said, not caring for Sean's attitude. "To answer your question, Mark found you. It didn't take long to scrub the data and find you."

"How?" Sean asked a second time.

"How? Mark and the NSA ran a search on your name. About 45 minutes ago someone named Josie Diaz posted a picture of you and her mother on Instagram next to a huge bouquet of flowers. I assuming they were from you. Lovely, by the way."

Sean gritted his teeth. He wanted to scream into the phone. "What can I do for you?"

"I assume you saw the news about the attack in Iran."

"Yeah, Colonel Farshid Shirazi was killed. Glad to see him gone."

"Correct. What you don't know is the whole op was executed without adequate intelligence and without Congressional approval."

"So what. That bastard was a terrorist."

"Sean, I didn't call to debate this. In approximately five hours Iran is going to launch a cyberattack of massive proportions, which will leave 70% of the country disabled. There's nothing we can do to stop it."

Sean let the phone drop and he looked at all the people in the room. He knew the chaos and death a loss of power, water and disruption of the food supply would cause.

"Hello? Sean?" O'Connor said from the other end of the phone.

Sean put the phone to his ear. "What do you need?"

"I need you on a plane. There's a small airstrip near Ontario. Be there in four hours."

"Not LAX?"

"The airports will be the first to go. You don't want to be near LAX. All aircraft will be grounded."

"Where am I going?"

"I'm working on it. Just get to the air strip."

Sean listened to the directions, hung up the phone and looked around. He felt sick to his stomach. He didn't want anyone here to be hurt. He didn't want Mrs. Diaz to have to endure the blackouts and the riots that would follow. Josie was closely watching Sean.

"Who is David O'Connor?" she asked Sean.

"Do you mind if I make another call?" Sean asked, ignoring the question.

"Go ahead."

## No Shortcut Home

Sean began dialing. "Please pick up," he mumbled under his breath.

"Hello?"

"Ana. It's Sean."

"Hi Sean, we were just talking about you," Ana said, elated to speak with him.

"Ana, I need for you to listen very carefully. David just called me. There's a cyberattack coming. You need to stock pile as much food, water and diapers as you can, and you need to do it now."

"Sean, are you involved?" she asked, with panic in her voice.

"This is real. Please go now. I'll be thinking about you. Kiss Michelle for me." Sean hung up. Ana was stunned but believed Sean. She raced into the other room to talk with her father. They were out the door in less than two minutes.

Josie had her arms crossed and was looking at Sean. Sean took her hand. "Listen, I have to go. I'm really sorry. I want you to do me a favor."

"Sure." She looked at him skeptically.

"I want you to get your brother, head to the store and buy as much water and as many canned goods as you can."

"What? Are you nuts?"

"No. Just please do it." Sean let go of her hand. "Please tell your mother thank you and sorry that I had to leave so soon."

Sean left the house. When he got to the sidewalk, he sprinted to his Jeep. He had to get back to the apartment building to make sure the Mr. and Mrs. Lomax were prepared.

## 11
## Sam's Wholesale Club
## 6PM – Los Angeles

Sean roared into the Sam's parking lot. He parked and opened the rear doors to the Jeep and lowered the seats. He jogged into the store. Out front were carts and flatbed carts. Sean grabbed two of the flatbeds, pushing one and pulling the other. He immediately headed over to the beverage section and began loading 5-gallon jugs onto the cart. He stopped at 10. He pushed the cart to the food section and added a couple cases of nuts, multiple cases of tuna, crackers, cookies, a 25-pound bag of rice, SPAM, peanut butter, canned fruit and canned vegetables. He threw baby wipes on the cart along with toilet paper, flashlights, a lantern and two cases of batteries. He added two boxes of bandages, Neosporin and two big bottles of hand sanitizer. The girl at the checkout counter thought he was nuts. The total was over $1,800. Sean paid in cash and accepted the help of the manager to get everything loaded into the Jeep. It just barely fit, taking up all of the cargo area and the passenger seat.

Lastly, Sean filled up the Jeep with gas at Sam's and sped back to his apartment. He loaded everything into carts in the garage and pushed them to the Lomax's apartment. He ran to his apartment, shut the door behind him, pushed the mattress off the bed exposing a small safe. He opened it and took out two stacks of cash - $10K each. He flipped through three passports and placed them on the floor next to the cash. There was Glock 26 with two clips. He placed those on the floor as well. Going to his closet, he pulled a small back pack out. He placed one stack of money and the passports in the bag. The remaining cash he placed in his back pocket and stuck the Glock in his waistband. He replaced the mattress and left the apartment jogging down the stairs to the Lomax's apartment. He knocked on the door. Mrs. Lomax answered.

"Sean! How are you?" She instantly could tell something was wrong. "Come in. Come in. What's wrong?"

Mr. Lomax got up from his chair. "Sean, are you ok?"

Sean realized he was out of breath. "The U.S. is going to be attacked tonight. I have to make sure you both are going to be ok!"

Mrs. Lomax placed her hand on Sean's face. "Sean, honey. It's OK. Nothing is going to happen."

"Are you on drugs, boy?" Mr. Lomax questioned.

"Stan!" Mrs. Lomax snapped. "Tell us. Tell us what's going on."

Sean took a deep breath. He told them who he was and who he sometimes worked for. Both of them were stunned.

"I have supplies outside for you. I don't know how long the attack will last, but our intelligence says it starts tonight. Most of the country will lose power and water."

"There will be riots," Mr. Lomax blurted out.

Sean looked at him, panicked. "Yes." Sean opened the door and pulled the first cart into the apartment, followed by a second, a third and then a fourth.

"Sean, this is a lot of stuff."

"I want to make sure you have enough and don't have to leave this apartment."

"Stan, where will we put all of this?" Mrs. Lomax asked.

"There's room in the second bedroom." Mr. Lomax answered.

Sean began to neatly stack everything up. He pushed the carts outside the front door.

Sean closed the door and stood in the Lomax's living room. "Please don't tell anyone you have this food. It will put you in danger. When I come back, we can donate anything you don't use to the food bank."

Mr. and Mrs. Lomax sat next to each other on the couch, still not fully believing Sean.

"How much cash do you have?" Sean asked.

"I think we have about $37 in the cookie jar."

Sean shook his head and pulled the stack of cash out of his back pocket. "This is ten thousand dollars. Keep it. You might need it." He put the money on the coffee table in front of the couch.

"Sean! We can't take your money!" Mrs. Lomax shouted.

"You need it and I have plenty." Sean reached behind his back. "Mr. Lomax, you were in the Air Force, right."

"Yes."

Sean pulled out the Glock.

"Sean! Get that out of here!" Mrs. Lomax shouted again. Her husband put his hand on hers.

"If you're asking if I know how to use it, I do."

Sean cleared the Glock and handed it and the clips to him. Sean then handed him the keys to his Jeep.

"The Jeep has a full gas tank. Take it if you need it."

"Sean, we don't know what . . ."

Sean interrupted them and pulled the small backpack tighter over his shoulders. "Mr. Lomax, how much insulin do you have?"

"He's got enough for nearly 8 weeks." Mrs. Lomax answered.

"Good. When the power goes out, Mr. Sanders needs to lock down the building. Seal the garage and all entrances. There are heavy gates that he can lock. Go tell him to do it, before things get out of hand."

"Thank you, Sean."

"Be safe."

Sean left the apartment and pushed the carts back to the garage.

## 12
## Blackout

Sean pushed the Ducati Panigale hard through LA traffic, weaving in and out. Prior to getting onto I-10, he stopped at a Jimmy John's. He had no idea where the plane was going or how long he was going to be in the air. Sean was constantly hungry. His metabolism ran like the Ducati he was riding, and he needed to keep filling his body with fuel. Sean hustled into the restaurant, ordered three "giant" subs, stuffed them in his bag and took off again. He didn't want to be on the road when the power failed. It would be instant gridlock.

Sean found the airstrip with no trouble. He could see a new Gulfstream G650 on the runway as he made his way down the narrow road leading to a couple of hangers. Sean parked the bike in the back of a hanger and walked out towards the jet. He climbed the stairs and was greeted by two pilots. Well, sort of greeted.

"You Sean?" one grunted. The second pilot didn't say a word.

"Yeah."

"Good. We're wheels up in five. Take a seat."

The plane was empty. Sean slid his bag off and took a seat in the middle of the plane.

"Good to meet you too," Sean mumbled.

The pilot slammed the door shut and started for the cockpit.

"Hey, where are we going?"

"I don't know. East is all we were told. We just need to get in the air."

"Ok." Sean made a face and tried to get comfortable. The plane immediately turned and shot down the runway. They were in the air instantly. Sean looked out of the window looking for the lights of LA. It was dark. The U.S. was already under attack.

It was 9:01PM local time.

## 13
## Panic at 1600 Pennsylvania Avenue.
## 12:01AM – Eastern Time

The White House had momentarily been plunged into darkness, until its sophisticated system of generators kicked in. The generators were the only thing running smoothly, however. President Robertson was asleep, having had too much to drink earlier in the evening. The Secret Service was scrambling, as was the staff.

The Joint Chiefs were on the way to the White House. Sloan Bennett walked into the residence with two Secret Service agents to wake the President.

The President was not happy.

"What the fuck are you three doing here?" he demanded, in the dark as was most of the U.S.

"Mr. President, most of our major cities have been hit with what we are calling a cyberattack." Sloan explained as the President got out of bed and stumbled across the room. "The Joint Chiefs recommend we move to DEFCON 3. This is serious."

"A cyber-what?" he asked, trying to get his hair into place.

"A cyberattack, sir. You might remember that Director O'Connor had warned us of Iran's capabilities."

The President spun around. "This is his fault!"

"Sir?"

"You heard me! Now go wait outside!"

The Chief of Staff left the Presidential bedroom and closed the door behind him.

Forty-five minutes later, the President emerged from the residence. Apparently, the country could wait while he made sure his hair was perfect. Bennett and the President walked through the White House, passing people staring at cell phones that no longer worked – all service had been disrupted.

Everyone stood, including CIA Director O'Connor when the President entered. President Robertson took a seat at the head of the table.

"Well?" he asked with a tone.

The Director of Homeland Security, Tim Blakely cleared his throat. "Mr. President, all of our major cities are without power and water. We have grounded all aircraft. No cell phone in America is currently operational. We estimate that in four and a half days, 68 percent of the population in every major city will be without food or the means to drive to find food. All gas stations are currently not operational."

"What? Don't we have a plan for this? Who did it?"

Blakely continued, "We are working to shut down all trains currently running. We have lost control of all switch yards."

"So?" the President blurted out.

"Mr. President, what this means is that they or whoever has done this can switch tracks and send trains off the tracks or create head on collisions." Blakely looked around the room. "The good news is that our chemical and nuclear plants have not been touched. We are working to secure our refineries."

"Who did this?!!!" The President screamed.

"Iran along with its proxies," the CIA Director calmly answered. The sound of David O'Connor's voice infuriated the President.

"What? They wouldn't dare after our show of force!" The President argued.

"It appears to have had the opposite effect." O'Connor responded. "In addition, our actions have also pulled the Chinese into this."

A general turned to O'Connor. "How so Director?"

"When we hit the building, a group from the Chinese oil ministry was in the building conducting a meeting. The grandson of the President of The People's Republic of China was killed."

Several "Oh, my gods." were heard in the room. The President stared at O'Connor.

"I now believe that tonight's attack was executed by Iran but with China's full knowledge." O'Connor added, knowing the Chinese were furious.

"Hit them back!" The President shouted as if he was playing a board game.

"That would not be wise," O'Connor warned. "The attack is being conducted from multiple locations. All of them outside of Iran. We are in the . . . ."

"Bennett! Get him out of here!" President Robertson screamed at the top of his lungs.

"Sir, he's the clear subject matter expert on this," Bennett argued. David O'Connor was already packing up his briefcase.

"As far as I'm concerned, this is his fault!"

The room watched the CIA Director leave the situation room. Sloan Bennett followed closely behind him.

"David! David!" Bennett called to O'Connor as he headed down the hall. The CIA director stopped.

"Yes, Sloan?" O'Connor calmly answered.

"I need you here. You and your team are the only ones that can solve this."

"What do you need for me to do? The President and his National Security Advisor have been undermining our work as an institution since he took office. I don't see how I can be of any help."

"Are you done with the martyr bit, David? Cause, I need you."

"Alright Sloan. What do you want?"

"Wait in my office. Once this cluster of a meeting is over, I want to talk. I know you saw this coming and have a solution. We need to make sure it's put in place."

O'Connor turned without a word and continued down the hall.

"So, is that a yes?" the Chief of Staff yelled.

## 14
### Isle of Skye – Scotland

Sean's plane touched down on a remote airfield. Sean looked out the window. The Isle of Skye was beautiful with rolling hills painted with a lush, calming green that Sean had never seen before. However, there was really nothing for miles. When the pilot opened the door, cold, wet air that smelled of salt filled the cabin. Sean's jeans and light jacket were not going to cut it here. He left the plane and walked towards the only two buildings for miles, a hanger and three-story building.

The building was worn from top to bottom and looked like it took a daily beating from the wind and salt air. Sean walked through the front door. Sitting at a table was Mark Phillips. Unlike Sean he was dressed for the climate. He had on a thick navy sweater, wool pants and boots. "Sean, come on in."

"Hey Mark. Where's David?"

"D.C.," Mark said getting to his feet. Sean shook Mark's hand.

"Good to see you, buddy. Great job finding me by the way."

"Thanks Sean. Don't be mad."

Sean looked around the room and smiled, "It looks like sweater season guys!"

No one laughed. Phillips shook his head indicating that Sean should shut up.

There were five other people in the room. Two Sean pegged as special forces. The other two looked like Mark - analysts. The last was a woman, who clearly was an intelligence officer of some sort.

"Sean, this is Colonel Jacobs and Major Sandsfield. They are with the SAS."

Sean shook their hands. "You cold?" Jacobs asked, elbowing the Major.

"Yeah, this is a little different than LA."

"We train up here! This is one of the good days!" Jacobs joked.

Mark continued the introductions. "These are our friends from MI6. Mitch Gabbert and Paddy Wilkenson. They're analysts. Lastly, this is Maggie."

"No last name?" Sean asked.

"No, Mr. Garrison. No last name," Maggie answered with a smirk.

"Great to meet you. I think." Sean answered. The SAS men laughed at Sean's response.

"You're not as dumb as you look, mate!" Sandsfield exclaimed.

"OK. That's enough. We have a lot of work to do and not a lot of time." Mark said while asking everyone to look at the small screen on his laptop. "Sorry, this is best I can do." He looked over at Sean. "Sean, come closer. You're the one that's going to be executing it."

Sean moved closer to the screen.

"This is a six-story office building eight miles outside of Reykjavik."

"Iceland?" Sean asked, sounding a little stupid in the process.

Everyone turned and looked at him.

"Yeah Sean. Iceland," Mark responded.

"Sorry. I just got here. Give me a break."

"As I was saying, after the attack on the U.S., we detected an extremely high level of internet activity emanating from a small area outside of Reykjavik. We were able to pinpoint everything coming out of this building." Mark stood up and pointed at a satellite image. "Based on all records we have searched; the place is still under construction and there should be no one there."

Mark flipped to another screen. "However, British satellites were able to pick up strong heat signatures from the building that indicate at least a room if not a floor of servers. In addition, we have been able to get a closer look at the building. Cameras and security. More than you'd see in an abandoned building." He then flipped back to the image of the building. "For this to work, we need to get in and out without being detected." Mark looked at Sean. "Sean, you'll need to land via parachute on the roof and enter the building from the door located here." Mark pointed at a rooftop door.

"The roof? By parachute?"

"A HALO jump, mate. You good with that?" Jacobs asked, staring down Sean.

"High altitude. Low Open. Sure," Sean answered, trying to sound confident.

"You've done it before, right?" Sandsfield asked, a little skeptical.

"Yeah. I'll be fine." He wasn't.

"Sean, we believe that the group that attacked us is part of a larger organization. The organization is made up of cells that are linked and located all over the globe. If they know we're there, we will lose the other cells. You need to get in and install this device into any server." Mark pointed to a device that looked like a small iPhone with a USB sticking out of it.

"Just find the server room and install this."

"I think it's on the fourth floor." Mark added. "We will be installing software and also extracting data. We need three minutes to get what we need. Then, you pull the device and get the hell out."

"To where?"

"Once we are in their system, we can manipulate the building cameras and security. We'll provide an alley for you to escape. They will never see you."

"Ok, sounds do-able," Sean answered.

"The building is surrounded by thick woods. You'll exit the building and head east for approximately three miles. There you will hook up with the major and the colonel and all three of you will get to a MI6 safe house in Reykjavík. I'll give you the exact coordinates for the rendezvous."

"When do we leave?" Sean asked, wanting to get this done and get back to LA.

"The SAS guys leave in one hour. You leave in three. Also, as you probably surmised, the British were not attacked. I'll be able to keep an eye on things via one of their satellites."

"Can I get something to eat?" was Sean's response.

Mark was anticipating Sean's need for calories. "Yeah, the kitchen is through those doors. Grab something and come back. I want to go through everything one more time."

Sean returned with sandwiches and a large bottle of water. He drank and ate while Mark went through everything again. Satisfied that Sean had it down, Mark nodded to the pair of SAS officers.

"Sean, let's get you geared up," the major said calmly. Sean followed both men into an adjacent room. There were two long tables with enough guns and knives to do some real damage. The room looked like it had been last painted in 1966. Likewise, the furniture looked vintage. It was a time warp.

"Take what you need. We weren't sure what you'd want so we brought a bit of everything."

Sean glanced at the table. He knew immediately what he wanted. However, his prolonged glance at the HALO (High Altitude -Low Opening) suit caught the attention of the colonel.

"Sean, you OK with this jump, mate? You look a little nervous."

Sean picked up the arm of the suit. "Yeah I'm nervous. I have to hit the top of the building and if I don't this whole thing is blown."

"But you've done it before?"

"Yeah." Sean lied.

"We have some time before we leave. We'll help you get your gear packed." The major packed the gear Sean selected and pointed him towards a selection of black combat fatigues and boots.

"Thanks guys."

"Don't mention it. Pints on you in Reykjavík," the major said, smiling.

Sean smiled while going through the gear. "That's a deal." Sean followed the SAS officers back out into the main room and sat down across from Mark.

"Any news?" Sean asked.

"Nothing good. Everything from water, to power to cell service is out in every major US city. It appears that the rural areas are not affected, at least not yet."

"What about LA?"

"Dark. The national guard has moved into the major metros to try and prevent riots, but it's only a matter of time before something erupts."

"How fast can we turn everything back on?"

Mark sat up in his chair and looked at the two analysts. "It depends. We have to see how much of a mess they made. A week? Hard to say." The analysts nodded.

"All this from one hasty decision."

"That's all it takes, Sean."

Sean abruptly rose, frustrated and not wanting to talk about it any further. "I'm going to grab a nap. I have a feeling I'm not getting any rest for a while."

Sean went back into the adjacent room and took a nap on a couch that was pushed up against a wall next to the HALO gear. He didn't feel like he'd been sleeping long when he felt someone watching him. He opened his eyes and found Maggie leaning against a table eyeing him.

"Time to go," she said. Maggie was about 5'8" with black hair. She wore grey wool pants and a thick ivory colored sweater.

Sean sat up and put his feet on the ground. "Thanks." He ran his hands through his hair and stared at the floor. He was waiting for her to leave. She wasn't.

"I'm getting dressed now," he said looking up at her. She stood in the same place, now with her arms crossed.

"Go ahead."

Sean shook his head and got up. He walked across the floor, pulled off his shirt, dropped his pants and began to put on the gear the SAS guys has left for him. He looked over his shoulder.

"This what you came for?" he asked with a little bit of a tone.

"Actually, yes. I wanted to get a look at "the" Sean Garrison."

Sean turned. "What's that supposed to mean?"

"I think you know." She said, moving to the couch, sitting down and crossing her legs.

"No, I don't think I do," Sean said shaking his head, a little aggravated.

"You know, I knew Robert Waters," she said casually, leaning against the arm of the couch.

Sean zipped up the black combat fatigues and turned, shirtless. Maggie took stock of the scars on his torso and shoulder. "Never heard of him" he snapped. Of course, Sean would never forget the man that sucked him into an off-books assassination program that forever changed his life, or ruined it, depending on the day.

"I met him when I first started out. I knew he was rotten. Evil to the core. He had no soul and seemed to be out to collect the souls of others. I hope he burns in hell."

"I couldn't say either way," Sean responded as neutral as possible, which was hard, given what had happened to him.

Maggie got up and stood in front of Sean. She ran her hand over the long scar across his chest while looking up at him. "For what it's worth, I'm sorry."

"Thanks."

"Sean, are you good with numbers?" she asked in a seductive voice, while retracing the scar. Sean was a little uncomfortable to say the least.

"Yeah."

"Remember this one. 3545982151."

"Why?"

"I thought we might get together." She winked at him and stepped back.

Sean didn't respond.

"Sean, what's the number?"

"3545982151"

Maggie stopped at the door.

"Good. Don't forget it."

Sean watched her leave. "I won't be calling her. I have enough crazy in my life," Sean mumbled and continued getting dressed.

## 15
## HALO
## 2AM local time.

Sean was alone in the back of the plane. It was stripped bare, with only a bench on each side. He was hooked up to the plane's oxygen, knowing that he'd need the small tank he was carrying when he jumped out at about 25,000 feet. He couldn't wait to shed the 40 plus pounds of jump gear when he hit the top of the building. Sean tightened the straps across his chest and adjusted the night vision goggles perched on top of his head. He was already cold and was preparing himself for the negative 30-degree air to punch him in the gut when the doors opened. Lights began flashing and the rear doors of the plane began to open. When they were down, Sean ran down the ramp and leaped into the cold night air. He figured that he should treat it like jumping into a cold pool – it's better to just jump in than to think about it.

The air was indeed a punch in the gut. Sean remained in free fall for the time the SAS team had prescribed. At approximately, 4,000 feet, Sean deployed the RA-1 Ram Air Free Fall chute. A navigation system guided Sean to the target. Sean pulled down and flipped on his night vision goggles. He could see the building in the distance. The roof was pitch black. There were lights on in the top three floors. Sean struggled to reduce his speed as the building got closer and closer. His feet scraped the edge of the roof as he landed. He thought he landed silently. He'd find out soon enough.

"Mark, I'm here," Sean said softly.

"Good. There are people on the top three floors." Mark said with the confidence the British satellites gave him.

"How many?"

"Hard to say."

Sean took off the parachute gear, wadded it up and looked around. There was a large HVAC unit to his left. He carried his gear over with the intent of hiding it in a vent or duct. When he came to the other side, he got a rude surprise.

"Huh, Mark. There's HALO gear on the roof."

"What??!!" Mark answered in a panic.

Sean was counting. "Twelve chutes. No markings on them."

On his end, Mark studied the satellite images. "Sean, I count 32 heat signatures. However, only 12 are moving."

"Shit," Sean said, carefully opening the roof top door. He knew the other 20 weren't taking naps. The stairwell was dark. He slowly entered the stairwell and peered over the railing. He didn't see or hear anything.

"Sean, get in and out."

"Duh," Sean answered, making his way down the stairs with his H&K G36K up and ready. He could hear voices on floors above him. It sounded like someone was tossing the place looking for something and seemed like an eternity to reach the 4th floor. Sean cautiously opened the stairwell door. The familiar hum of computer servers greeted him. There was one fluorescent light on near the door and the room was semi dark. There was a body in front of him, face down. Sean stepped over him and walked down the rows of servers, to the third row and followed it to the end of the row. He pulled out a small flashlight to find a USB port. Slipping off a small backpack, Sean pulled out the device Mark had given him. He flipped it on and plugged in the USB. A small light flashed.

"You're in."

"Sean, you did it. Great connection."

"You've got three minutes and I'm getting the fuck out of here." Sean stood up and took a deep breath. He looked to his left and saw a second man face down. It was then he heard a familiar voice. "I know that voice," he said to himself. Sean kneeled down. There was a small tablet in his right hand. Sean turned it over. On the screen was a video of the President of the United States in one of his clubs bragging to a group of men about taking out Iran. The men all laughed. One man with a big cigar shouted, "You must look strong!" Sean recognized the accent. It was Russian. Then the screen went dead.

"Damn it," Sean whispered. He tried to get it to open but failed. He looked at the dead guy, lifted his dead hand up and placed his thumb on the screen. The tablet unlocked. Sean placed the tablet in his pack and pulled a knife out of his vest.

"Sorry, buddy." Sean thought, as he cut off the man's thumb and placed it in his bag. Sean put the pack back over his shoulders.

"Mark, you have 30 seconds." Sean stood and pressed his back against the servers. A door opened on the far end of the room. Sean could see a man dressed exactly like him, looking at an image on a phone. He pushed the dead body by the door over and held the phone next to his face. Then he spoke. It was Mandarin. He was reporting that he hadn't found "him."

"They are Chinese," Sean whispered.

"What? How do you know?" Mark questioned.

"I speak Mandarin. Idiot."

"How many men? You have 10 second left," Phillips answered, ignoring Sean's comment.

Sean didn't respond. The Chinese commando was walking down the aisle toward Sean. He tried to press himself further against the black server, trying to be invisible. He pulled his knife. The Chinese commando straddled the body with Sean an arms-length away. He rolled the man over and compared his face to the image on the screen.

"I found him." He relayed in Mandarin to his team. Sean thought he was going to walk off, but he stopped. He noticed the missing thumb. When he turned, Sean jabbed the razor-sharp blade into the commando's throat, grabbing the back of his neck at the same time to drive the blade through his larynx and into his spine. The man collapsed on the floor next to the thumb-less hacker.

"Mark. I really need to get out of here."

"Go. We have what we need."

Sean pulled out the device and ran for the stairwell.

"Where are they?" Sean asked, opening the stairwell door carefully.

"They are on the sixth floor but look like they are headed for you."

Seeing it was clear, Sean took off for the ground floor and the exit.

"Mark, do you have control of the cameras yet?" Sean was now at the emergency exit on the ground floor. He was getting nervous and didn't want to die in Iceland in a cold stairwell.

"A couple minutes."

"Mark! I can hear them in the stairwell! I'm leaving! I don't give shit about an alarm at this point."

"Sean wait! They stopped on three. They are exiting the stairwell."

"I hear them. There's something outside." Sean explained as calmly as he could.

One of the MI6 analysts tapped Mark on the shoulder and pointed at a monitor.

"Sean, we're picking up at least 14 men in the woods on the edge of the parking lot."

"14? Are they in front of the door?"

"Directly across from your exit point."

Sean slid down the wall of the stairwell. He checked the H&K G36K. He jumped at the sound of gun fire.

"Sean! Sean! They are shooting at each other! The Chinese are engaging the men in the woods! You have a window! Go! Go!"

Sean burst out of the door and headed right, away from the fire fight. A dozen or more rounds struck the building just above his head. Sean didn't stop and ran flat out across the grass along the side of the building through the parking lot and jumped over a line of shrubs into the thick woods. He didn't slow down and ran flat out for nearly a mile. Branches scraped his face and arms flew as he ran through the pitch-black woods.  He finally stopped, leaned up against a tree and took a deep breath.  He was alone for the moment.

## 16
## White House Kitchen

CIA Director O'Connor was sitting at a table in the massive White House kitchen talking with the White House chef. He'd gotten tired of the Chief of Staff's office. O'Connor was enjoying a freshly baked apple pie and glass of milk when Sloan Bennett walked in.

"There you are." Sloan said, out of breath and with an awful look on his face.

"You've had me here all night."

Bennett ignored him. "David, a bit of a break. The NSA, working MI6 have think they have the key to locate the holes in our system and get everything back on line. It's going to take a while - maybe a week to restore power and water to most of our large cities. It could have been worse."

Bennett took a seat across from the CIA director.

"Have some pie, Sloan."

"David. I'm also here to tell you you're fired. I'm sorry." Bennett looked at the CIA Director studying his face. "You're not surprised about either thing."

David O'Connor took another bite of pie. "Not really. We have good people working here. The President has not been able to run them all off yet. I knew they would prevail. And, I knew it was only a matter of time before I was fired."

"You can give me your letter of resignation. I'll give it to the President."

O'Connor placed his fork on the edge of the white presidential dinnerware and wiped his mouth. "Sloan, there will be no letter. I want everyone to know I was fired. Frankly, I'm disappointed the President didn't do it himself."

"He doesn't like to do that."

"I know." David O'Connor stood and looked at the White House Chef. "Chef, a masterpiece! Thank you! The best pie I have ever put in my mouth."

The chef waved at the CIA Director. "You're so welcome!"

Sloan Bennett walked David O'Connor out of the White House.

## 17
## Oval Office
## Same Time

The President was sitting at the Resolute Desk watching his National Security Advisor pace the room.

"O'Connor was running an unauthorized op without either of us knowing. We were running around like idiots while he sat here in the White House with that snug little look on his face."

"Bennett just fired him," the President answered.

The phone on the President's desk rang. He ignored it. An instant later, a staffer knocked and entered the Oval Office.

"Mr. President. Ambassador Larianov is on the phone."

The President waved the staffer off and waited for her to leave before answering the phone.

"Mr. Ambassador. We're quite busy here as you probably know."

"Mr. President we have another problem."

"What's that."

"The hackers that just attacked your country have a video of you, me and your club members discussing the attack on Colonel Shirazi and the fact that you were aware of the presence of the Chinese when you . . . ."

The President shot to his feet. "WHAT!"

Paul Doolittle approached the President's desk, trying to hear.

"A little over an hour ago, one of your men breeched a building in Iceland that we had under surveillance and made off with the video. Our forces on the ground were unable to stop him."

"FIND HIM!!!" The President slammed the phone down on the desk.

The Russian ambassador conveniently left out the Chinese involvement on the ground in Iceland. He didn't want the President knowing that the Chinese were after the video as well. Larianov then placed another call to his team in Iceland.

"What happened?" Doolittle asked, clearly beginning to panic.

"O'Connor's op. Stop it now!"

"Now?"

"Did I stutter! Shut the fucking thing down!!! And lose the transcript of that last call!!!"

Doolittle left the room at a slow jog. He entered his office and called his contact at MI6 that had leaked

Sean's op.  He demanded the plug be pulled immediately.

## 18
## Isle of Skye

Mark Phillips and the two MI6 analysts stared at the monitors in front of them. Mark was trying to help Sean make it out of this in one piece as he raced through the woods. A phone on the edge of the table rang. The MI6 guys ignored it, but it kept ringing. It would stop for a few moments and begin ringing again.

Sean was running through the woods as fast as he could. There were no paths, it was dark and the forest was thick with trees. The night vision goggles helped – a little.

"Sean, you should be half a click from the SAS team. They are waiting."

"Copy." Sean tried to double his pace. He wanted out of there. He came to the top of a small hill and could just see both SAS officers leaning against the front of a black Land Rover. They were dressed as civilians. The other side of the hill was a little more treacherous than it looked. He took the decent slowly. He reached the bottom and was 40 meters from the Land Rover when he saw Sandfield's head snap backwards, spraying the windshield with blood. Jacobs didn't have a chance either. A second round split Jacob's head in two and he slumped to the ground in front of the truck.

"Fuck!" Sean said, falling to the ground. He landed in a shallow puddle of black water and wet leaves. The water was ice cold. Cold is better than dead. He lay there motionless. He had no idea where the shots had come from.

"Mark. Mark. They're dead! There's a sniper." There was no response from Phillips. "Hello?"

Mark Phillips lost contact with Sean. "Sean? Sean?" There wasn't an answer. Then the monitors went dark. The pair of MI6 analysts looked at each other and then at Mark.

"That's not good," one stammered.

"What bloody happened!" Maggie shouted from across the room, striding towards the monitors. "Get these damn things back on! We have three men out there!"

"Try to reboot it!" Mark ordered.

The phone rang again. This time one of the analysts picked it up. "Hello." He answered timidly. Talking to people was not his favorite thing.

"This is Miles Chamberlain. Who am I speaking with?"

Maggie began waving her hands telling him to not answer.

"Nigel."

"Nigel who?"

Maggie smacked her hand against her head and mouthed "stop talking!"

"Bakersman."

"Well mister, you're in some hot water. This is an unauthorized op. I don't know where you are, but you need to be in my office in London first thing in the morning. In the meantime, you'll write down everyone involved in this boondoggle and send it to me straightaway."

"Yes."

Maggie took the phone from his hand and hung it up. Both analysts were freaking out. "Nigel, it will be fine."

"Fine? That guy reports directly to the PM!"

"He's a hack. I'll take care of you guys. I always do. Get packed up."

"That's it? We have three men out there. Sean is being chased by what sounds like special forces units from two different nations." Mark said, raising his voice

Maggie remained calm. "Mark, I'm going to take care of it."

"How?"

"I'll handle it." Maggie said, trying to reassure him while she wracked her brain for a solution. She needed all three to stay alive for a few more hours until she could get on the ground in Iceland.

## 19
## Muddy Ditch in Iceland

Sean quickly realized something was wrong and he gave up trying to hail Mark. He was on his own. He remained motionless in the puddle. The cold, wet leaves stuck to his face as he focused on trying to spot the sniper. There was no movement in the forest. He knew the sniper was waiting for him. Sean glanced at his watch. It would be dawn soon and he'd be screwed. He kept an eye on the truck. It was beginning to become light outside. He was shivering and his feet felt numb.

About 20 meters in front of him, a dark figure emerged from the forest. The sniper moved carefully, sweeping the area as he made his way to the Land Rover. He looked inside and then leaned his sniper rifle against the passenger door. He stood in front of the truck, rolled over Sandsfield and began searching him.

Sean figured this was his chance. He got up and silently covered the distance to the Land Rover and crouched behind the truck.

"They're clean. Nothing on them. No ID either. Neither is the man we're looked for," the man reported in Russian. The sniper walked to the side of the truck to retrieve his rifle. At the same instant, Sean pivoted from around the back of the truck and put a suppressed round through his head. The sniper fell to his knees and then on his face. Sean rolled the man over. There was nothing on him to identify who he was. Sean kneeled down and pulled out his knife. He had a good guess who this guy was. Sean pulled the men's jacket open and ripped his shirt apart with the knife, exposing a chest full of tattoos.

"Damn it! He's Spetsnaz. What the fuck are they doing here?" Sean said aloud, rising to his feet and placing the knife back in his vest. Sean looked around and then went to the front of the truck. Sandsfield and Jacobs died horribly. Sean felt sick to his stomach. "I'm sorry guys. I'm sorry," Sean said as he dragged each man into the forest by his pant leg and gently placed them next to a tree. Sean did the same with the sniper, but without the pleasantries.

Sean returned to the truck. The windshield was covered in blood. He pulled his helmet and goggles off and tossed them into the truck. He removed his tactical vest and threw it on the floorboard. He noticed the duffle the SAS team had prepared for him with a change of clothes. Sean started the truck and ran the windshield washers for a moment and drove off. He had at least two special forces teams after him. So much for an easy in and out. He drove for a few minutes down a dirt road until he hit the service road next to a highway, merged onto the highway and followed the signs to Reykjavik.

Sean drove for 20 minutes and saw a sign for a petrol station, pulled into the station and circled the parking lot, looking for a place to change and ditch his gear. The station was not full of people, but it wasn't empty either. He scanned the lot for cameras. Most were trained on the pumps. Two large trucks were parked in the back. Sean pulled between them and got out. He stripped off his clothes and dressed in the civilian clothes from the bag, pulled on a black baseball cap down over his face. He wiped the remaining black face paint off as well. There was nothing identifying on his gear, but he checked anyway. He scanned the parking lot looking for a dumpster to trash his gear. He did see that the back of the truck parked next to him was open. He pulled the hatch and stuffed his gear in a box right inside the door. Satisfied, he got back in the Land Rover and packed the knives, the H&K and the Glock in the large duffle. Sean opened his backpack. The tablet was not damaged during Sean's run through the wood. The bloody thumb was resting at the bottom of the bag. Sean pulled out a zip lock bag containing cash, credit cards, a Canadian passport and Canadian driver's license in a simple black wallet. He started the Land Rover and left the lot. He was going to have to ditch the truck and do it soon but for now he needed it and got back on the highway.

At the same moment, a Russian GRU officer was scrubbing CATV footage and spotted the Land Rover. He couldn't get a clear look at Sean's face, but was able to determine the direction he was headed. He contacted the team on the ground. Their target was 30 minutes in front of them. The officer, now knowing where Sean was headed, turned his feeds to all cameras between the petrol station and Reykjavik.

Sean was not a fool. He knew cameras were his enemy and that the Russian and Chinese had more than likely tapped into every camera in Iceland. He kept his hat low and tried keep his face obscured.

Unfortunately, he was right. The Chinese had located him and had a team pulling into the petrol station he had just left.

At the moment, neither team could identify him. That was a break for Sean.

Sean gripped the wheel tightly. He was desperately looking for a place to ditch the truck and the H&K G36K. Keeping the weapon seemed like a good idea at first but now it was a liability.

After five or ten minutes, Sean ran across a Straeto station. There were dozens of buses at the station. It was the best he could do at the moment. He drove past the station and pulled the truck into a parking lot. He parked the truck at the far end of the lot. He grabbed the duffle and pulled his hat down low. He noticed a storm drain in front of the Land Rover. He looked around, crouched down and pushed the H&K into the storm drain. Avoiding the cameras as best he could, he boarded a bus and was soon on his way to Reykjavik.

The Chinese and Russians scoured the camera feeds but could not find Sean.

## 20
## White House

With each passing moment, the President became more and more anxious. The Russians couldn't determine who Sean was and couldn't locate him. The President reminded the Russian Ambassador that it would be his ass as well if that video saw the light of day.

"Doolittle, this is O'Connor's man! That fuckin' old coot, is out to get me! Find out who this guy is!"

"Sir, I have been trying. No one at the agency knew about this op."

"Sure they didn't! They have all been against me since I stepped into this office," the President barked, pacing the floor.

"MI6 has also been a dead-end. They don't know the identity of the agent. In fact, Mr. President we can't even assume that this guy is an American. He could be anyone."

"Is that supposed to make me feel better?"

"No sir." Doolittle stood motionless, staring out the window of the Oval office.

Sloan Bennett entered the office. He stopped in his tracks when he saw the body language of his boss and the NSA. He cleared his throat.

"Mr. President, we need to discuss Iran. The Joint Chiefs will be here in an hour." the Chief of Staff reminded.

"What about?" the President said absently.

Bennett was a little shocked at the answer.

"The attack. They are denying everything of course. There's also the matter of our assassination of the head of their intelligence services."

The President took a deep breath. "Come get me later. We're dealing with something right now."

Bennett left without a word. He fully realized that he should never have taken this job.

Inside the Oval office, Doolittle wracked his brain for a solution.

"We know the guy is still in Iceland. Surely, the Russians can track this guy down."

The President leaned against the Resolute desk. "You'd think."

"We could haul O'Connor in here . . ." Doolittle suggested.

The President stood up and pointed at his NSA. "I like it. Haul him in here."

"I'll call the AG." Doolittle answered.

"Yes! And tell him to do this right now. I mean right now!"

Doolittle left the room to call the AG. The President sat back behind his desk and stared out of the window.

## 21
## The streets of Reykjavik

Sean stepped off the bus. It was around 9AM local time. He needed to do a couple things fast. He needed a new set of clothes, food and most importantly, he needed to secure the video he was carrying. Sean could see a handful of shops down the block. He found a café without much effort and went straight to the café's restrooms. He locked the door and washed his hands and face, removing the dirt and the remaining face paint. He took out the tablet and the hacker's severed thumb and turned on the device. He watched in shock. It was a crystal-clear video of the President spilling national security secrets and doing it for profit. The video was indeed shot from the camera of one of the President's cronies in one of the President's gun clubs. The phone had been expertly hacked and accidently placed in the ideal place to capture everything. It was a one in a million shot. Sean turned up the volume and leaned against the sink watching. The President was front and center in the video. There was no mistaking that it was him.

President Robertson: "You boys want a huge stock tip?"

Unidentified man #1: "Always!"

President Robertson: "I've decided to take out most of Iran's intelligence leadership."

Unidentified man #2: "I'll make sure I take a look at my holdings. Definitely a chance to pick up some money."

Unidentified man #1: "What about you Mr. President?"

President Robertson: "Oh, I'll make some on this."

Off camera Sean heard a voice with a thick Russian accent.

Russian man – unidentified: "You must look strong! Mr. President, this is a bold and decisive decision that will project strength. I applaud you!"

Everyone claps. The President smiles, loving the attention.

Russian man – unidentified: "May I have a word with you alone, Mr. President?"

President Robertson: "Boys, meet me in the bar."

The room is now empty, the Russian steps into the frame of the video. It's the Russian ambassador. However, Sean doesn't recognize him.

Russian Ambassador: "A little tip. If you happen to wait until Tuesday, the Chinese oil minister will also be in the building."

President Robertson: "So?"

Russian Ambassador: "The grandson of the Chinese President will also be there."

President Robertson: "I hate that bastard. This tariff shit is out of control."

Russian Ambassador: "I just thought you'd find this information useful."

Then the video ended.

Sean stood looking at the tablet. No wonder the Chinese and Russians were after this video and him. A loud knock at the door made Sean jump. He stuffed everything back into his bag, put it over his shoulder and left the men's room. He stood in the doorway thinking about what he needed to do and where he needed to go. He determined that a coffee would help him think and so would food. He ordered and sat down. The café was half full. It looked like any other café he'd been in around the world. Then his brain started working.

"Damn it." he said aloud. He had wasted 5 minutes. When he powered up the tablet, it had connected to the Wi-Fi in the café. He wagered that the tablet was now being tracked. He opened his backpack and unlocked the tablet using the severed thumb. He placed the tablet on the table, opened up a browser, found an email service and created an account. He then uploaded the video to an email and then left the email in the draft folder. Sean hoped that this kept the file safe. He logged out of the email account and began taking apart the tablet. He got the sim card out and broke it in half. The rest of the tablet was a little tougher. He thought about smashing it on his chair but knew it would make him memorable should anyone come looking. Sean got up and went to the men's room. He locked the door, took out the hacker's thumb and flushed it down the toilet. He placed the tablet on the floor, leaning against the wall and smashed it with his foot. It burst apart. The smaller pieces went into the toilet as well. Sean held on to the larger tablet components, left the café and tossed the parts into a series of trash cans as he moved up the block. He stopped at the next intersection and looked back at the café. Three large, unpleasant looking men were entering the café. They looked like Russian GRU. Sean turned and headed up the street, keeping his hat down over his face and avoiding cameras as much as possible.

## 22
## David O'Connor
## Langley, Virginia

David O'Connor was calmly packing up his office when he heard a knock at the door. He turned to see two men in navy suits, white shirts and ties. He put the box he was holding down on his desk.

"I'm going to guess you gentlemen are with the FBI," O'Connor said, in a slightly mocking tone.

"Yes. I'm Special Agent Anderson and this is special agent Baker."

O'Connor walked behind his desk and continued packing. "What can I do for you?"

"We'd like for you to come with us," Anderson said, walking into the office. Baker stood by the door.

"Oh? Where? And why?"

"We'd like to ask you some questions regarding the cyberattack. We'll be going to the Hoover Building."

"No."

Both agents looked shocked. "No?"

"Am I under arrest?"

"Not currently," Anderson responded.

# No Shortcut Home

"That's a curious response, Special Agent Anderson," O'Connor responded while picking up his phone. He looked up at the agents. "I'm calling the director, just so you know."

The phone rang several times and FBI Director Bob Wallace picked up. "Hello David, I thought you'd be calling."

"Bob, I have two of your men standing here wanting me to come in for questioning."

The FBI director cleared his throat. "David, I resigned an hour ago. That's all I can say."

"Over what?"

"You. That's all I can tell you. We'll catch up. Good luck David." The now former FBI Director said and hung up. O'Connor placed the phone back on the desk and looked at the agents.

"Gentlemen, I am choosing not to go with you." O'Connor said, pulling on his suit coat and staring down the two FBI agents.

"Sir, coming with us voluntarily will be easier on you."

"I've been the Director of the CIA for a long time, guys. I'll take the hard way."

The two agents shook their heads and left the office. David O'Connor watched them leave and then shut the door to his office. He went back to his desk and picked up a secure line and dialed Mark Phillip's phone. Based on the appearance of the FBI, he was betting Sean had stumbled into something bigger than a group of hackers.

"This is Mark." His voice was full of panic. "The Brits pulled the plug . . ."

"Mark, calm down," O'Connor said trying to calm him down.

"Where's Sean?"

"He might be dead, David. We lost contact with him. I think we lost him."

"Slow down. Tell me what happened."

"When Sean arrived at the building, a Chinese special forces team was already there."

"OK."

"You don't seem surprised."

"No."

"A second special forces team was in the woods and engaged the Chinese, which gave Sean the window to escape," Phillips explained.

"Who were they?"

"I'm not sure."

"Are you still in the UK?"

"Yes. Heading to Heathrow."

"I want you to stay there. Things have gotten a bit nasty here. The President fired me, and the FBI Director resigned. I don't want you flying home to this," O'Connor said, placing more pictures into the box.

"OK. I'll stay put."

"Oh, and Mark, I wouldn't worry about Sean. He's going to be very tough to kill. Based on the reaction from the White House, he's still alive and appears to be giving at least two world leaders fits.

## 23
## Grimur Hotel
## Reykjavik

Sean picked up a change of clothes and checked into the first suitable hotel he encountered. The Grimur Hotel was across from a bus stop and a shopping center, which would make it easy for him to blend in. He thought the hotel looked like a two-story elementary school. He used his Canadian passport and credit card to check in and got a suite next to the fire escape on the second floor.

He tossed new clothes on the bed, closed the shades and double checked the door and security bolt. His heart was pounding. He'd been running for seven hours straight. He turned on the shower and let the hot water run. He pulled off his clothes, threw them in the bathroom's trash can and got into the shower and let the water run over his body. He washed the remaining face paint off that was caught up in his hairline. There were still a couple of rotting leaves on his chest. They circled the drain. He dressed and sat on the edge of the bed. He needed to get out of Iceland and back to the U.S. He still had not decided what to do with the video. The more he thought about it, the more his blood began to boil. First thing he needed was food. He left the room, ordered two sandwiches from the restaurant and two beers. While he was waiting for his meal, he noticed two men watching a rugby match at the bar. Sean walked over and stood nearby, pretending to watch. What he really was interested in was the cell phone left sitting on the bar. He walked up next to them and ordered a beer and stood there watching and waiting for his chance. His meal gave him the opportunity he needed. The bartender placed the bag containing Sean's food next to the phone. He picked up the bag and phone and left the bar. He brought the food to his room and dug into the food.

"What was that number?" Sean mumbled. He paced the floor for a moment and then began entering Maggie's number. It took two attempts, but he finally got her.

"That took long enough." Maggie answered.

"Where are you? I need to get the hell out of here," Sean said, running his hand through his hair.

"Sean, you need to tell me where you are," Maggie said calmly.

"Iceland."

"Sean, I know that. I'm in Reykjavik right now. Tell me where you are."

Sean continued to pace, trying to decide if he trusted her. He finally relented. "Meet me in an hour."

"OK. Where?" Maggie asked patiently, knowing that Sean's nerves were probably fried.

Sean stormed over to the coffee table where a tourist magazine caught his attention.

"The Saga Museum."

"Hmmm. OK Sean. See you there."

Maggie hung up. Sean destroyed the phone. He sat down on the couch and finished his meal while flipping through the magazine. He pulled a cartoon map out of the magazine to figure out where the Saga Museum was. Realizing it was 6.2km from the hotel, he tossed the magazine across the room. He leaned back and closed his eyes. After a moment of feeling sorry for himself, Sean got up, checked the Glock 26 he still had in his possession, stuffed it in his backpack, pulled a black wool cap over his head and left the hotel. He quickly found a bus heading where he needed to go. After sitting down, he realized riding the bus was the smartest thing he could have done. It was packed and he blended in.

## 24
## Saga Museum
## Reykjavik, Iceland

Sean stepped off the bus 100 yards from the museum. He was 30 minutes early for the rendezvous with Maggie and that was OK. He entered the museum, paid and began wandering around. The museum struck Sean as a well-done wax museum and, like the bus, it was packed with people. Sean followed a tour group, again trying to blend in. He kept his eyes open looking for large, angry looking Chinese intelligence agents and former Spetsnaz – now GRU - they'd be easy to spot.

Sean identified Maggie shortly after she entered the museum. She had on tan slacks, a grey sweater and a black pea coat. Sean watched her make her way through the museum. Her eyes scanned every inch of each room she entered. She stopped and was intently examining the Leifur the Lucky exhibit. Sean walked up behind her.

"I was wondering when you'd get the courage to say hello," Maggie said, as she turned and faced Sean.

"Maggie, I'm so sorry. I couldn't do anything to save your men," Sean whispered, getting closer to her.

"Sean, I know. We can talk about it later. You are radioactive. Everyone is looking for you. The good news is no one knows your name and best I can tell they only have a vague physical description. You've done a great job staying off camera."

Sean looked around. "Did you speak with Director O'Connor?"

"You don't know, do you?" Maggie said as she picked up Sean's right hand and caressed the back of his hand and then his fingers.

"Know what?" Sean asked, concern climbing into his mind.

"Your President fired him."

"Shit. I'm in deep trouble."

Sean then noticed Maggie touching his hand. "What are you doing?" She ignored him.

"Technically, I'm not supposed to be here. MI6 pulled the plug on us. Someone from the President's staff made a call and killed the op."

"Well, that sucks. I can't stay here. I have to get back to the U.S."

"What did you find Sean?" Maggie asked, getting closer and placing her hands on his chest.

Sean pushed her away slightly. "Nothing," he answered in an incredibly unconvincing fashion.

## No Shortcut Home

"Don't lie. I can tell you are really bad at it," Maggie said, with a sideways smile and gazing up at Sean. Sean and Maggie moved to the side of the exhibit to allow people to take pictures.

"Nothing." He said trying to emphasize that she'd didn't want to know. Maggie suddenly took Sean's hand and began leading him out of the museum.

"We're leaving."

"Great. Where?"

They began walking away from the museum. Maggie led Sean down a narrow lane to a black BMW. The engine was running. Maggie stopped a few feet from the BMW and once again took Sean's hand.

"Sean, I want you to trust me. There's no way I can put you on a plane. Commercial or private. They will have you in a heartbeat."

"Then how am I getting out of here?" Sean looked off at the ocean in the distance.

"A boat," Maggie said, waiting for his reaction.

"OK. Why not?" He said sarcastically, throwing his hands in the air.

"There's a cruise ship leaving in the next hour. It will take you to Dublin. From there, you will catch a plane to Ottawa. From there, you're on your own."

"How long on the boat?"

"Four days."

Sean rubbed his hand across his face and looked off into the distance again. "Won't they catch me there?"

"No! Highly unlikely. Plus, I have had one of our guys fool around with security alerts at Husavik Airport. They will be arresting someone matching your description in the next 30 minutes. Husavik is halfway across Iceland."

"There's food and beer on this boat?" Sean said slyly.

"All you want and I have booked one of the best cabins on the ship," Maggie said, playing along.

"Alright. Let's go. Thank you, Maggie."

Maggie smiled at Sean as she reached for the rear passenger door. "You're welcome." She opened the door. "Oh, and there's one small thing."

"What's that?" Sean asked.

"Everyone is looking for a lone man. Not a couple."

Sean nodded thinking, Maggie was coming along. Sean started to get into the back of the BMW, noticing a set of long legs partially covered by a plaid wool skirt.

"I think you guys know each other," Maggie said and started laughing.

"Well, if it isn't Sean Garrison!"

In the back seat sat Natalia Molotov. Sean froze halfway into the car.

"Nat." Sean stammered, slowly closing the door behind him. Nat's wool skirt and a tight black top were expertly matched to accentuate her figure. A coat was folded neatly next to her. Her dark hair was now blonde, which she wore down, cascading over her shoulders. She looked very much like her cousin Ana. However, Sean wasn't about to mention that.

Maggie got into the driver's seat and took off.

"Looks like you're in a lot of trouble." Nat said with a huge smile on her face.

"Yeah." Sean whispered, sitting as far from her as he could. "How did you know I was here?"

She reached over and touched Sean's leg, leaning towards him. Her ice blue eyes cut right through him. "This is going to all work out and I'm going to make sure you're able to do whatever it is you need to do. I'm not going to ask what it is and I don't want to know." She sat back up.

"You didn't answer my question, Nat." Sean asked cautiously. He was stunned to see her. He'd reached out to her nearly every week for months. He didn't know if she was dead or alive. He realized he was in love with her, but naturally became frustrated. He'd thought he was over her, but seeing her again made all of those feelings come rushing back. Sean still sat pressed against the door with his hand on door handle.

"No, I didn't." Nat said and made a confused face at Sean, looking at his hand on the door handle. "You're not planning on jumping out, are you?" Maggie laughed and looked at Sean in the rearview mirror. She was teasing him and making him feel like a fool. Sean didn't answer her.

"So, Maggie, what do you think?" Nat asked.

Maggie looked in the rearview mirror at Sean again. "You're right. He's kind of hot."

Nat smiled and looked at Sean out of the corner of her eye. "Yeah, kinda."

Sean slumped in the seat. Getting captured by the Chinese sounded preferable to this.

Maggie pulled the BMW into a small parking lot adjacent to the port.

"Sean, I'll need whatever weapons you're carrying," Maggie said calmly. Sean knew there was no point in lying. These two would see through him in a heartbeat. Sean placed the Glock on floor of the BMW.

"Maggie, thank you." Sean said, leaning forward and placing his hand on her shoulder.

"Thank me by not getting killed." Sean smiled a weak smile and got out of the car. Nat was standing by the trunk.

"Sean, would you mind getting these bags." With the tall black boots she was wearing, Natalia Molotov came eye to eye with the 6'3" Sean. She slid on a pair of sleek black leather gloves. Sean pulled two heavy bags out of the BMW's trunk.

"Yes dear." Sean answered sarcastically. The trunk was barely closed when Maggie hit the gas and took off out of the parking lot. Sean and Nat made their way to the cruise ship.

## 25
## Cabin 427
## North Atlantic

Maggie was not kidding about the cabin. It was a large suite with a king-sized bed, a balcony and decent sized bathroom. Everything from the linens to the pillows to the down comforter were a blinding shade of white. Outside the cold North Atlantic looked formidable. Sean plopped down on the loveseat and watched Nat as she unpacked one of the suitcases.

"You need two for this trip?" Sean said with a tone.

"One is for you, silly." Nat replied, smiling and ignoring Sean's nasty tone. "You need clothes. I think I got the size right."

"I'm sure you did." Sean stretched his legs out and continued to observe Nat. She'd walked out on him and now suddenly appears when he's in need. It was too weird.

Nat put a gown on a hanger and looked over her shoulder at Sean. "You really should take a shower."

Sean pulled at the cheap shirt he'd purchased in Iceland and sniffed. He didn't reply, got up and went into the bathroom. He emerged five minutes later to find his clothes folded nicely for him on the bed. Without a word, he picked up the clothes and went back into the bathroom. The clothes fit perfectly. In fact, Nat knew his sizes better than he did. When he came back out of the bathroom, she was sitting on the couch sipping a sparkling water and smiling at him.

"Still don't drink?"

Nat took another sip and shook her head, "no".

"You don't mind if I do?" Sean really wasn't asking permission and was being a little bit of a pouty jerk. He crossed the small room and began to open the mini-fridge.

"I've got you covered," Nat said holding up a cold glass containing a beer. Sean shut the fridge door and turned around.

"Am I that predictable?" He said taking the beer and sitting down next to her.

"Yes, but for your sake, it appears that I'm the only one that's figured you out," she said a little bit smugly.

"Nat, why did you leave? I just don't get it," Sean said as he turned towards her on the loveseat. Nat gently grabbed his shirt and pulled him towards her delivering a long kiss. Sean went along with it. He liked it and wanted more, but his brain woke up. He stopped kissing her.

"Nope. Nope. You're not going to do that," Sean said, pulling away.

"Do what Sean?" She said innocently.

"You have me wrapped around your little finger. I want to know what's going on." Sean stood up and moved to the edge of the bed across from her. "Look, I care about you and I think you feel the same about me. Why did you just vanish?"

Nat stood and straightened her skirt. "Sean, there are some things I'd rather you not know." She faced the balcony window. Sean made a confused face.

"What? That's your reason? I don't see what it could be. You do know about all the awful things I've done. I can't see what it is. I want you to trust me, Nat," Sean said changing his tone and speaking in a softer voice.

"I do trust you Sean. You're one of the few people I do trust." She put her drink down and kneeled in front of Sean and placed her hands on his knees, looking up at him. "Sean, I love you. I think I fell in love with you the moment I met you in the casino in Vegas." She blurted out.

She began crying.

Sean took her hands and lifted her to her feet. "I feel the same about you. I have since we met." He brushed her blonde hair away from her face.

She smiled, "I think you just wanted to sleep with me," she laughed a little.

"I think you have it backwards. You spent most of your time trying to seduce me."

"Maybe . . . ." she said and kissed Sean lightly on the lips.

"I'm clearly the one with the self-control," Sean said sarcastically.

Nat laughed. "Yeah, that's your number one personality trait."

Sean kissed her again. "Do you want to check out the ship?" he asked, picking up the sweater on the bed and pulling it over his head.

"I was kind of hoping we'd stay right here," she said with a smile.

Sean, always a little slow when it came to these things said, "Well, I already put on the clothes you brought me. We could go get a drink."

"I never said you had to put them on."

"Oh! I see what you did there. I like that idea," said Sean now catching on.

Nat put her arms around Sean's neck and kissed him. "Good thing you're pretty."

"I get that a lot," Sean answered.

"No, you don't."

## 26
## Dublin
## Cabin 427

Sean sat on the bed as Nat neatly packed her bag. She periodically looked over at him and smiled. Sean was watching the BBC, learning that things in the U.S. were slowly getting back to normal. However, the west coast of the U.S. was still without power or fresh water. President Robertson had escalated tensions by sending the Fifth Fleet from the Indian Ocean toward the Persian Gulf. The Seventh Fleet was also preparing to head toward the Middle East. Thankfully, France and Germany were working overtime to cool tensions and head off another war in the region.

Nat laid a navy suit and a white shirt on the bed. Naturally, she was dressed in a flattering, long black skirt and tight red top, which made her look even taller and despite her beauty, intimidating.

"You don't expect me to put that on do you?"

Nat made a face indicating that Sean was an idiot for asking. "You're going to. Do you want to look like a man who is on the run, in nasty clothing or a professional on his way home to Ottawa?"

"When you put it that way, it makes more sense," Sean said sheepishly and began to dress.

Sean and Nat left the cabin and headed down the hallway to disembark. Sean realized he had spent four days with her and still had no idea how she knew he was in trouble, who sent her and from a personal standpoint, why she took off. He'd loved every minute she was with him and she indeed had him under her spell.

There was a black Mercedes waiting for them. They headed for Dublin Airport. Nat held Sean's hand in the back seat, turning his hand over periodically to trace the lines on the palm of his hand. As happy as he was, Sean knew she was taking off again.

The car pulled to the curb. Nat handed Sean his ticket and turned towards him. "Sean, thank you for this time together. I know it was not ideal, but worth every minute. I'll never forget it."

"This sounds like you're not coming."

"I can't."

Sean was disappointed but tried not to show it. "You're always there for me. I just don't want this to end."

She leaned over and planted a long kiss on his lips. "Go."

Sean opened the door without another word, gathered his bag and headed into the airport.

Nat wiped a tear from her cheek and watched him enter the airport. She tapped the back of the driver's headrest and the car took off from the curb.

## 27
## Ottawa
## Fairmont Chateau Laurier

Sean had settled into the Fairmont, just steps from Parliament Hill. The trip had been incident free. Maggie's plan had worked perfectly. The Fairmont has a famous bar called Zoe's. Sean had seen the bar when he checked in. The place was too cool not to visit and grabbing a drink was too tempting. It was a little after 8PM and he was heading out for the U.S. in the morning. One drink couldn't hurt. Sean grabbed a seat in the middle of the bar. Sean ordered a beer and the Lady Laurier Burger. At $34, it was the most expensive burger he'd ever had, but worth every penny. The place was full of lobbyists and staffers from Parliament. He watched them push and shove at the bar and laugh at each other's horrible jokes. Still dressed in his navy suit, Sean blended in. The bartender took Sean's plate and delivered a fresh beer. He didn't notice and older Chinese gentleman take a seat next to him. The man ordered a scotch and quietly sipped on the drink, staring straight ahead. Sean caught a glimpse of him in the bar's mirror. He was dressed in a tweed jacket and blue dress shirt and a simple tie. His black hair more grey than black. He wore a pair of wireframe glasses that gave him a scholarly appearance. After a few moments the man spoke but didn't turn towards Sean.

"David says you're a good man," he said in Mandarin.

Sean nearly choked on his beer. He looked up at the man and then spun in the chair, expecting the room to be filled with a Chinese special forces team.

"It's just me."

Sean cautiously turned around and took another sip of beer. Sean replied in Mandarin, "That's interesting."

"In fact, he said he could always count on you to do what was right no matter the consequences."

"How do you know David, if you don't mind me asking?"

The man took a sip of his scotch and stared straight ahead. "He's been my friend for 45 years."

"He's a good man as well," Sean replied.

"So, is he correct?" the man said, placing his drink on a napkin. Sean turned his beer glass in counter clockwise circles as he thought about everything that was being said. He had a feeling it would either lead to his immediate death or keep him alive to live another day.

"He is," Sean said, turning towards the man. "And you can rest assured I'm going to do the right thing now."

The man finished his drink, placed some cash on the bar and stood. "Then you have nothing to fear from the People's Republic of China."

He left the bar.

Sean let that last part sink in for a moment. It seemed like good news, but he didn't want to wait for a Russian to sit down next to him and order a vodka. Sean paid his check and headed straight to his room.

## 28
## Buffalo
## Amici's Ristoranti

The BMW Motorcycle dealer in Ottawa was happy to see Sean. He bought a BMW K 1600 GT without so much as a test ride, paid cash and then bought a jacket, gloves, helmet and boots. Sean loved the big bike. It had loads of torque, could fly and was comfortable. He liked his Ducati back in LA, but this big bike was so smooth, he felt like he could ride it for days. The 350 miles to Buffalo were flying by. He was stopped at the U.S. border and entered with no trouble. He arrived in Buffalo hungry, as always.

He found a cool Italian place, Amici's Ristoranti and parked his bike outside along the curb. When he opened the door, he knew he'd found the right place. The restaurant smelled amazing. It was almost full. Sean stood in the waiting area and studied the pictures on the wall. They showed a happy family doing what they loved, making great Italian food and being with each other. He noticed the name Ippolito pop-up on a couple of photos. It made him realize that he'd lost touch with his friend, Brian Ippolito. Brian was still a cop in Pittsburgh, now engaged to a great girl and doing great. He needed Brian's calm demeanor back in his life.

"Right this way sir." A pretty hostess showed Sean to a table in the back.

"Thank you," Sean said, as he took the menu from her. Sean being Sean began to order more than the average person. Everything was good. Toward the end of the meal, the owner, Ezio stopped by the table. He was a handsome guy, that clearly loved what he did. Sean could tell by the way he interacted with his staff and the guests.

"I hope everything was excellent" Ezio asked.

"Perfect. Everything was perfect." Sean answered. "I saw there were a couple people named Ippolito up on the wall by the hostess stand."

"They are my cousins," Ezio explained.

"My best friend back in Pittsburgh is named Ippolito. Great guy."

"I'm sure he is," Ezio answered. "I'll tell you what, dessert is on me. Any friend of an Ippolito deserves a free dessert."

"Thank you. You don't have to do that."

Ezio laughed. "It's the least I can do, you've eaten easily over $90 worth of food on your own. Thank you for coming in tonight."

"Well, it was amazing! Thank you."

Sean enjoyed his dessert, taking his time. He was glad to have the Chinese off his back. The public needed to see the video he'd obtained in Iceland. It couldn't be buried, and he was going to make goddamn sure it wasn't. It was then he scraped plans to head to New York City. He had originally planned to take the video directly to *The New York Times*. But now he had a better idea. He was going to hand it off to the newly elected congressman from Idaho and former Delta sniper, Mike Richardson. Mike would do the right thing.

He'd be heading to Washington D.C. in the morning. Sean paid and left the restaurant.

## 29
## Java Steve's
## Washington D.C.

Mike Richardson was easy to find, and Sean quickly saw that he was a creature of habit. Up at 5AM. Run. Stop at the coffee shop at 6:10. Run home. Shower. Head to the Hill. For two days, Sean jogged behind Mike, watching him, but also making sure that Sean was not bringing any heat down on a friend. On the third day, he decided to just go straight to the coffee shop. Mike never saw him. Sean sat in the middle of the coffee shop with a baseball cap on reading *The Washington Post*. Deciding the time was right, Sean approached Mike. It didn't appear that Russians, or the FBI were going to fly through the front door. At this point, Sean believed that there was a better than average chance the FBI was also looking for him. He knew David O'Connor was being interrogated by the Justice Department and knew David would never give him up. Mike walked into Java Steve's and went straight to the counter to order. There were 12 or 13 people in the coffee shop. Most were staring at computers or their phones. Sean had noticed that Mike seemed to have a thing for one of baristas but based on his behavior he had not asked her out.

"May I take your order?" the barista asked. She had a homemade name tag that read "Becky" which she had clearly created using letters from the newspaper. She was blonde, about 29 years old and liked eagle tattoos. Not the potential girlfriend a former Delta sergeant and freshman congressman would typically go for.  Sean liked her however.

"Just a large black coffee."

She looked at him.  "I know you, right?"

"It's Mike." Mike said, slightly stammering.

"Cool."  She wrote his name on the cup.  "That's $3.25."

Sean walked up behind Mike.  "I'll get that Becky." Sean handed her a $10.

"Oh, hi Sean!  That's sweet."  Becky, the barista responded.

"Keep it."

"Thanks Sean!"

Mike spun around excited to see Sean.  He shook his hand and gave him an awkward hug.  His excitement turned to worry very fast.  "Dude, I love seeing you, but I know seeing you here like this can't be good."

"Mike, I love seeing you too."  Sean slapped him on the shoulder and ignored the comment for the moment.  "Congress!  I'm so excited for you!  Proud too!"

"Thanks Sean."

"Foreign Services Committee and Armed Forces Committee, right?"

"Yeah, very good, Sean," Mike answered, cautiously. He looked Sean up and down. Sean blended in with everyone in the coffee shop. He had on a grey hoodie and black shorts and a hat. He looked like he could be anybody. This made Mike even more nervous. Sean was on the run.

Becky handed Mike his coffee and looked at the name on the cup. "Here you go, Mike. She then looked at Sean and smiled. "Thanks Sean."

Sean smiled back.

"And why am I not surprised that she already knows your name?" Mike asked, looking back at Becky as he spoke.

"I'm polite," Sean answered. "Let's sit down." Mike followed Sean to a table in the rear of Java Steve's.

"You didn't answer me, why are you here?"

"I need your help."

"Sean, you know I'll do anything for you. I wouldn't be here if it wasn't for you."

Sean sat with his back to the wall and studied Mike's face, re-thinking if he was making the right call involving Mike.

Mike took a sip of his coffee. "Well?"

"Let me see your phone," Sean asked with his right hand out.

"Why?"

"Just give me your damn phone." Sean snapped. Mike handed Sean the phone. Sean typed for a few moments, finally placing the phone on the table and sliding it to Mike.

Mike could tell that Sean was serious. He left the phone on the table. When the video of the President started, he quickly looked around and then back at the screen. Sean studied his face as he watched. After the video ended, Mike stared at the phone.

"Where did you get that?" Mike asked, leaning forward.

"From the hand of a dead hacker in Iceland."

"Shit."

"Yeah Mike. Shit." Sean answered.

"You ended the cyberattack."

"No smart people did. I just helped." Sean looked around. "And I've been on the run ever since I jumped out of the plane. The Russians want me dead. O'Connor was fired and is being questioned."

"What do you want me to do?" Mike asked.

"I want you to make this public."

"WHAT?" Mike blurted out.

"Yes," Sean calmly answered.

"That's the President of the United States! The head of the party!"

Sean sat stone faced. "All correct. And you'll do it in 24 hours, or I take this to *The New York Times.*"

"Sean, my career will be over before it even gets started."

Sean started to get up. "I think I've made a mistake."

Mike grabbed his arm. "No."

"Mike, I thought you were more than this. This is bigger than your party affiliation."

"Sean, come on, sit back down."

"Fuck that Mike. You took an oath and I know it sure as shit wasn't to that guy in the White House."

"Fuck you, Sean."

"I know you came to D.C. to serve your country just like you did in the Army. If all you accomplish is to expose this epic corruption, you'll have done more than 99% of the pricks on the Hill."

# No Shortcut Home

Mike leaned back in his chair and exhaled.

"You're an asshole, you know that?" Mike said.

"So, I've been told."

Suddenly, Sean was all smiles. Becky came to the table.

"Sean, I brought you a fresh coffee."

Sean smiled big. "Thank you, Becky."

Mike glared at him.

"It's no problem" she answered, smiling. She turned to leave.

"Hey Becky, this is my friend Mike."

Mike sat up in his chair.

"Hi Mike." She smiled at him. Actually, it was kind of a half-smile - one that was only half interested.

"Mike is a U.S. Congressman." Sean said proudly. "He'd never say it. He's too modest, but I'm not. I'm proud he's my friend."

"Wow! That is so cool," Becky said, suddenly interested.

"Thank you." An embarrassed Mike answered.

"You know, Mike's office is having a reception later this month. You should come," Sean said, glancing at Mike. "We'll send you an invitation."

"Really! I'd love that!" Becky responded, now happy to know Mike. "See you soon." Sean watched her walk back behind the counter.

"Laying it on a little think don't you think?" Mike exclaimed, shaking his head.

"Not really."

"Oh. And I'm not having a reception this month," Mike said.

"Then make one up," Sean replied.

"I don't have her number," Mike whined.

Sean spun around his cup around to face Mike. Becky's number was written in purple marker on the top of the cup in a playful script.

"I hate you."

Sean got up and patted Mike on the back as he walked by.

"I love you, buddy. 24 hours."

Sean walked out of Java Steve's and broke into a fast jog down K Street.

## 30
## U.S. Capital
## Mike Richardson's Office
## Next Day

Mike's limited staff had reached out to all of the major networks and print media to try and get them there for his press conference. Mike had for all intents and purposes lost the office lottery and had scored one of the worst offices in Congress. No one ever wanted to come by his office. In attendance, there was a junior CNN reporter (only because she liked Mike) and a couple of print outlets, but it was sparse to say the least. No FOX. No MSNBC. No *Washington Post*. Mike's team rolled out a large monitor. At exactly noon, Mike stepped up to the mic.

Mike was visibly nervous. The CNN reporter smiled at him. Mike cleared his throat.

"I'm not excited to be here today and I'm not proud of what I'm going to share with you, but I will tell you that I will fight to investigate corruption no matter where it takes me or how high it goes. I realize that this might be my first and my last term in Congress and that's OK. I came to D.C. to serve my country, just like I did in the U.S. Army. I took an oath to the Constitution and not to a political party and I intend to live up to that promise." Mike gestured to the screen. "This video was given to me by an intelligence source. It was recovered during the operation to end the cyberattack that our country endured just 10 days ago."

Mike pushed play. As soon as the President's voice was heard and his image appeared, the reporters went nuts. They were instantly on their phones. The CNN reporter nearly spit out her gum. Her camera man struggled to keep the camera steady. She told her producer to get her on the air. Reporters were running down the hall towards Mike's office. Reporters were shouting for comment. Mike and his staff were overwhelmed.

A handful of miles away, Sean was sitting in restaurant eating Singapore noodles, drinking hot tea and watching Mike. "Good job Mike," Sean said to himself. He was planning to head over to Tyson's Corner to visit Pavel Fetisov. Pavel served with Sergei in the Red Army and after the death of Nat's father had adopted her. He'd know where she was. The server placed a bag of leftovers on the table. Sean paid and stepped on to H Street. There was a homeless person, covered in a navy-blue blanket sitting near the entrance to the restaurant. Sean, handed him the bag of leftovers.

"Here you go buddy," Sean said. The man didn't say anything but nodded. Sean had not gone five more feet from the man when someone pushed a taser into his neck. Sean passed out and started to fall. Two strong hands picked him up and pushed him into a black van. The doors closed and the van sped off.

## 31
## Oval Office

"What the hell??? Who is this guy and where the fuck did he get that video!!??" President Robertson screamed, throwing the television's remote across the room and jumping up from his desk.

Sloan Bennett cleared his throat. "He's a freshman congressman from Idaho."

"Get the Speaker of the House on the phone!! He needs to put a stop to this! We control both houses of Congress for Christ's sakes!"

"I have already done that. The Speaker was just as surprised as we are," Bennett replied as calmly as possible.

"He's clearly against me! Find something on him! Find it now!"

Bennett adjusted himself in his seat. "I can't and he's not against you."

"Are you blind?! Did you see what he just did??!" the President screamed.

"He's voted with you 89% of the time. He's also a veteran."

"So what!"

"And a decorated veteran with rock solid Pentagon connections. He was a member of Delta and considered one of their very best when he retired. The Speaker says he could be the future of the party."

"This has O'Connor written all over it. He should be in jail and so should this congressman!"

"Sir, the FBI has not had any luck with O'Connor. He's refusing to cooperate."

"Then get the interim FBI Director on the phone for me. Now! I'm going to take care of that CIA rat!" The President sat down behind his desk. "And, I don't care how wonderful this bastard congressman is. If there's nothing on him, then make something up and do it now!"

Bennett stood up, holding the stack of folders and binders he always seemed to be carrying. "No. I won't do it."

"Excuse me??" the President answered, clearly not used to hearing the word "no".

"Find someone else. I'm not smearing this guy," Bennett said, his voice getting stronger with each word that leapt from his mouth.

"Fine! Get out. Consider yourself fired." The President hit a button on his phone. "Get me Doolittle." He looked up at his former Chief of Staff. "This guy will get it done."

Sloan Bennett felt as if a weight had been lifted off of him. He left without another word.

**32**
**The streets of our nation's capital**

A huge man sat in the back and laughed looking at Sean's lifeless body on the metal van floor. Sean's head bounced off of the van floor as the driver sped through D.C. The driver looked over his shoulder at Sean. In Russian he asked, "You sure this is the guy?"

"Positive. He was seen talking to the congressman."

"Vladimir, who the fuck is he?" the driver asked.

Vladimir was going through Sean's wallet. "Driver's license says he's Canadian. Sean McManus from Manitoba. That's bullshit." He tossed the license and wallet on the floor.

"We'll squeeze it out of him when we get to the garage."

The van drove for another 20 minutes, finally pulling into a wet, pothole filled alley. They stopped the van in front of a garage.

"Damn door won't open!" the driver shouted over his shoulder.

"What?"

"I think the clicker is broken. It won't open." Both men got out of the van.

"Will you give me a hand with him," Vladimir asked. The driver came around to the back and pulled Sean out by his pant leg. Both men hoisted Sean up on either side and carried him toward the door adjacent to the garage. Vladimir fumbled with the keys to the door. Finally, he opened it.

"Turn on the lights!"

"I'm trying."

Vladimir flipped on the lights to find a woman sitting in a chair with her legs crossed, pointing a suppressed weapon at them. Before they could speak or even move, Natalia Molotov put a bullet into each of their heads. The men fell on top of the unconscious Sean. Nat kicked the Russians to the side and knelt down to check Sean. He was breathing but out cold.

## 33
## Tip Top Cleaners
## Tyson's Corner

Sean started to wake. Slowly, he sat up on a couch. Whose couch, he didn't immediately know. He was in an office. The couch was across from an old wooden desk. The walls were filled with pictures. Sean focused one picture in particular. It was a picture of a young Natalia Molotov on a ski lift. She was dressed all in black with ski poles in one hand. A big smile. Drop-dead gorgeous. He realized he was in one of Pavel's dry-cleaning locations. He knew he was safe. He leaned back and felt his head. He had a large knot on the side. A little dried blood came off on his hand. His neck also stung where he was hit with the taser. Better than dead. The door knob rattled a bit and Pavel walked in. He was dressed as he always was. Suit. French cuffs. Spit-shined shoes.

"Sean, my boy!" Pavel said in his big, accented voice.

Sean stood and hugged Pavel.

"How are you feeling?" Pavel asked, leaning back against the desk in his office.

"My head hurts." Sean said rubbing the side of his head. He sat back down. "Thank you. I'm not quite sure what happened, but I'm certain nothing good was on the horizon."

"It wasn't me." Pavel said, holding his hands out and shrugging.

"Nat?" Sean surmised, rubbing his hands on his pants, slightly embarrassed that she'd bailed him out again.

"Yes, great guess."

"Where is she?" Sean asked, knowing she'd taken off again.

"Not here." Pavel answered. He crossed his arms. "I tried to get her to stay."

"I know you did." Sean looked sad as he spoke. Pavel noticed.

"Look Sean, she's very complicated. Just give it time."

Sean nodded. He was clearly uncomfortable. "So, where did I screw up?"

"Ahhh that. You did really well up until that very last day. The Russians aren't dumb, they have been watching Mike for many reasons other than the video. Then out of nowhere, you show up. They don't know who you are, but you fit the description of the man who parachuted into Iceland. They were going to torture the truth out of you."

"They still don't know who I am?"

"No clue."

Sean stood up and paced the room. "So how did Nat figure it out?"

"She picked up a communication between field agents and their station chief here in DC. She followed the two gentlemen that snatched you."

"Where are those two now?"

Pavel made a face at Sean. Sean realized it was a dumb question. Nat didn't mess around. They were dead.

"I'm lucky to have her watching over me."

"Indeed." Pavel cleared his throat. "She's lucky to have you as well. Not many people can handle her, and she's never felt the way she feels about you."

"Pavel, then why does she constantly take off?" Sean said, standing in front of Pavel.

Pavel put his hand on Sean's shoulder. "It will work out. I know it will."

Sean shook his head. "I want it to."

"Are you heading back to California?"

"Yes, I think I've done what I need to do here."

Pavel looked at the TV mounted on the wall. A cable news network was on. Mike was being interviewed. "I'd say you've done plenty. Mike is going to be very busy."

"I knew he'd do the right thing."

"He always has. Brilliant move handing the video off to him."

Sean realized he had no idea where he was. "Pavel, I need a ride. I have no idea where I am."

Pavel let out a huge laugh that shook the pictures on the wall. He reached into his pocket and pulled out the key's to Sean's bike and tossed them to him. "You're in Tyson's Corner. I had your bike towed here. It's around back."

"Thanks Pavel."

"You're welcome Sean." Pavel hugged Sean and walked him out.

## 34
## Back in California

The power was back on in Los Angeles. After getting in, Sean's first stop was to check on Mr. and Mrs. Lomax. Sean knocked on the Lomax's door. Mrs. Lomax opened the door and threw her arms around Sean.

"Thank god you're ok!" Mrs. Lomax half shouted.

"I'm glad you guys are alright." Sean said, slightly uncomfortable.

"Who is it?" Mr. Lomax called from inside.

"It's Sean!" she answered over her shoulder.

"Ask him in!"

"Come on in, Sean."

Sean walked into the apartment and looked around. He could see the boxes of food stacked in the Lomax's second bedroom. He clearly had over bought.

"Take a seat, Sean." Mr. Lomax offered, pointing at the couch. "Boy, you weren't kidding. The power went out here and people went nuts. No power or water for nearly 10 days."

"No issues?" Sean asked.

"None thanks to you. We had plenty of food and still have enough for months," Mrs. Lomax replied.

"Good. Can I help take some to the food bank or did you want to keep it?" Sean asked.

"You can take the SPAM! I don't want to see it again!" Mr. Lomax answered from his recliner.

"I'll take care of it."

Mr. Lomax stood up, walked across the room, opened the top drawer of a desk and took out the Glock Sean had given him. He handed it to Sean. "Here. Glad we didn't have to use it." Sean took the weapon, cleared it and placed it behind his back in his waistband.

"I'm glad too."

"Oh! I almost forgot. Your money!" Mrs. Lomax walked across the room and into the kitchen and returned with the money Sean had given them. She started to hand it to him. Sean put his hands up.

"That's your money," Sean said shaking his head.

"Sean! This is a lot of money. We can't keep it."

"Yes, you can. You both keep telling me that you want to go on a trip. Take it."

Mrs. Lomax stared at the cash and looked at her husband.

"Mr. and Mrs. Lomax. Keep it." Sean said a second time.

Mr. Lomax realized they were not going to change Sean's mind. "Thank you, Sean. You're so kind to us. We will take that trip."

Mrs. Lomax hugged Sean again. "Thank you, Sean."

"You're welcome."

Sean left the Lomax's and returned to his apartment. He was getting tired of being alone. He laid back on the bed and stared at the ceiling. He needed to figure out Nat. He needed to figure out Ana. He missed his daughter. He also couldn't sit still. He decided to head over to Ollie's.

## 35
## Ollie's

Sean loved the speed bag too much. He got lost in it too quickly. He sat down on a bench to take a break. His arms and shoulders were burning. He took a long drink of water and began unwrapping his hands. From across the gym, Carlos Diaz was strutting towards him. He was back in his black trunks, hands wrapped, clearly getting ready to spar. He stopped a few feet from Sean.

"Where you been Sean?" Carlos asked with his hands on his hips. Sean leaned back and looked up.

"Travelling."

"How did you know we'd lose power?" Carlos asked, adjusting his feet. He was clearly uncomfortable.

"Lucky guess."

"Shit. It wasn't luck." Carlos sat down on the edge of the bench. "Move!" Sean scooted over. Carlos leaned forward, rested his elbows on his knees and stared at the floor. "We all thought Josie was crazy when she ran out of the house and came back with a truck full of food and water." Carlos looked up at Sean. "Sean, you really saved us. My mom would have really struggled."

"She's awesome. Glad you guys were ok." Sean answered, wanting the conversation to end.

"Look, I don't say thank you very well or as much as I should."

"You're welcome."

"Damn it! I didn't say thank you yet!"

"You're welcome." Sean answered again laughing.

"You're fucking with me, aren't you?"

"Yeah." Sean said, removing the wraps and stuffing them in his bag. Carlos stood up.

"Two things." Carlos said, hands back on his hips.

"What's that?"

"I'm saving two ring-side seats for you. My fight is in three weeks in Vegas."

Sean was excited. "Thanks! I wouldn't miss it." Sean picked up his bag. "What's the other thing?"

"A favor."

"Shoot."

"I need a sparring partner."

"You're nuts. No fuckin way," Sean answered. "Is this some way to even the score?"

"No. I'm serious," Carlos pleaded. "My trainer says I need to work with someone fast with a long reach. That's you Sean."

"Are you serious?"

"Yeah. You up for it?" Carlos said, rocking back and forth.

Sean thought for a few seconds. "I'll help but you've got to take it easy on me."

"No," Carlos answered without hesitation

"When do we start?"

"Now. Let's go," Carlos said, walking toward the octagon. He looked over his shoulder. "If you need a date for the fight, let me know. I have a really nice cousin."

Sean laughed. "Do I really look like I need help with a date?"

"Yeah. You do."

## 36
## Fight Night
## Las Vegas – MGM Grand

The arena was filled and rocking. Carlos was not kidding about the seats. They were ringside. Sean found Mrs. Diaz and gave her and Josie a hug, assuring them that Carlos was going to cruise to a win. He'd rented a tux. It took him nearly 30 minutes to remember how to tie a bowtie but managed to do it and not miss the fight. He took his seat and looked over at the empty seat next to him. He'd sent an email to Nat and also had left a voicemail on the only number he had for her. Getting her to Vegas was a longshot. Sean heard a whistle and turned his head slightly. A tall blonde dressed in a long black gown was heading down the aisle towards the ring. He did a double take. He thought it was Ana at first. It was Nat. Sean stood as she approached. She planted a long kiss Sean's lips.

"You thought I was Ana, didn't you?"

Sean blushed. "No. That's crazy."

"You're a bad liar." She sat down. Sean took the seat next to her. "You know, I almost told her to take the ticket." Sean gave Nat a look. She elbowed him. "I'm teasing you."

"Thanks for coming. I've missed you," Sean whispered into her ear. Nat squeezed Sean's hand as he spoke and placed another kiss on his lips. From across the arena, Sean could see Josie Diaz giving him a thumbs up.  Evidently, she thought he was hopeless as well and was thrilled to see Sean with a date.

"So, this guy has been beating on you for the last month?"

"No!  I was brought in as a specialized sparring partner."

"Ok. Ok. Calm down."  Nat laughed.  "I'm glad you didn't kill him."

The fight went back and forth for the first two rounds and it was clear that Carlos' work with Sean had paid off.  His opponent was taller and much faster, but at the end of the day, Carlos' tenacity and training prevailed.  He took the belt in three rounds.  The Diaz family was elated.  Sean was happy to have Nat with him.  They spent the weekend in Las Vegas and Sean convinced her to return to Los Angeles with him.

## 37
## LA
## "No Quarter"

Nat had spent the better part of a week with Sean. They'd attended a party celebrating Carlos' win and Nat met Mr. and Mrs. Lomax, who made a big deal of Sean in front of her. She told Sean she loved his tiny apartment, which was a small lie. She understood his aversion to technology but encouraged him to at least get a small TV. Sean didn't ask how long she was staying, he decided to just enjoy having her there.

"Sean, can I take your bike – the BMW? I need to go do a little shopping," Nat said standing in the kitchen, pouring a sparkling water into one of the three glasses Sean owned.

"Don't you want the Jeep?"

"No, I want to take that bike. I've been wanting to ride it since I got here. I can't believe you rode it here from D.C."

Sean picked up the keys to the BMW and tossed them to Nat. "It was a breeze. Have fun. I'll go grab something to cook for dinner." Nat snatched the keys out of the air, kissed Sean and left the apartment.

33 minutes later, Sean left the Save-a-lot with two bags of groceries. He'd found a nice bottle of wine to go with the Sea Bass they had in the meat department. He was walking back to the Jeep and

didn't notice the four men leaning on it. Sean slowed when he saw them. They were members of the same gang that he's fought outside of Ollie's.

"You think you're pretty fuckin' great, don't you?" one of the men shouted as Sean approached. Sean wasn't armed. His Glock was locked under the seat of the Jeep. The four men slowly surrounded him. It was clear they had weapons.

"You stuck your nose into something that doesn't concern you!"

"I have no idea what you're talking about," Sean answered, searching for a way out of this.

"Josie Diaz is my property. I can sell her. I can kill her. She's my property!"

"I'm not sure who you guys are," Sean answered.

"We're the 70's bitch!" a man shouted from behind Sean and then shoved him.

"Carlos just doesn't up and leave. Once a 70, always a 70! Carlos and I became 70's at the same time." He spit at Sean's feet after he spoke.
"We're going to make an example of you. You're going to remember the name Roberto Flores!"

"Look, I don't want any trouble from you guys."

"Fuckin' A you don't, but you've got it." Flores got up in Sean's face as he spoke. "I thought about killing that old couple you talk to all the time or burning down the shelter where you work and killing all those little puppies and kitties you love so much."

Sean dropped the groceries and shoved Flores backwards.

"Easy bitch!" Flores said, lifting up his shirt, exposing a silver pistol. Sean looked to his left and right. The other men had their weapons in their hands. "Yeah, we know all about you, Sean! All about you!"

Sean felt the rage he kept buried start to bubble up. He didn't see a way out of this, however.

"Hand me that fucking phone." One of the men tossed Flores an android phone, said a few words and then turned the phone to face Sean. On the screen was Nat on the BMW. She was being filmed from behind by members of the 70's who were following her in a van.

"What the fuck!" Sean stepped towards Flores. He felt the cold metal of a pistol on his back.

"You sit there and fuckin' watch."

The man behind Sean was driving the muzzle hard into his back. He was close enough for Sean to smell his breath – a mix of weed and cheap beer.

"Leave her out of this." Sean pleaded.

Flores smiled a nasty smile, filled with malice and brought the phone closer to his face. "Kill her."

"No!" Sean lunged forward. The man behind him hit him across the back of the head. He fell to his knees. Flores held the phone out. On his command, the van accelerated and struck Nat from behind launching her into a parked Nissan Maxima on the side of the road. The bike hit the trunk and Nat was sent flying over the car and into a telephone pole. Her lifeless body slid down the pole and hit the ground. Sean could hear the men in the van laughing.

"Now it's your turn," Flores said, nodding at the man behind Sean. The man placed the muzzle at the base of Sean's skull, but stopped. He looked up and past Flores.

"Five O!" On the edge of the parking lot, two LA County Sheriff's Deputies entered the center. All four men scrambled away, got into a van and started to pull away. Flores leaned out of the window, "We're not done!" he threatened as they pulled away.

Sean leaned forward on his hands and knees. The deputies got out of their vehicles and raced to Sean. One leaned down. "You ok sir?"

"They killed her! They killed her!" Sean stammered.

"Who?"

"My friend. They killed her. They ran her over!" Sean shouted.

"Are you injured?" a second deputy asked Sean. Sean began to get to his feet. The deputy helped Sean and steadied him.

"No." Sean was looking around the parking lot for Flores and his crew. "You need to help her!"

"Who?" the deputies asked, hands on their weapons. Sean was acting erratic and was a big individual that they didn't want to tangle with.

"She was on a bike. I'm guessing near Melrose. You have to do something!" Sean said, the panic rising in his voice.

"Check it." One of the deputies walked to his car and picked up the radio. Sean watched the deputy's body language. It wasn't good. He walked back to Sean and put his hand on Sean's shoulder.

"There was a fatality on Melrose and Highland. Hit and run."

"Oh my god!" Sean fell to his knees sobbing. The deputies tried to pick him up. Sean pushed their hands away.

"Look, we don't know if it's her."

Sean stood up. "It's her. I have to go." He pulled the Jeep's keys out of his pocket.

"Whoa! Sir, you need to come with us."

"I'm not." Sean left the groceries and got in the Jeep and headed out the back of the parking lot. The deputies let him go. He reached under the driver's seat and pulled out the Glock. He was five minutes from the Save-a-lot headed towards the accident scene and didn't notice the red pickup truck come up on his right. It slammed into the side of his Jeep, sending it careening over the curb on the left side of the road. A minivan pulled up immediately and the side door opened. Two men with masks opened fire with automatic weapons on the Jeep. Sean was quick enough to bail out of the driver's side door. He laid down behind the left front wheel, hoping the engine block and axel would provide some cover. The gun fire tore the Jeep to pieces. Soon gasoline was running under the Jeep. There was a pause as the two changed magazines. Sean sprung to his feet and got one shot off. It found its mark and hit one of the gunmen in the chest. He toppled out of the van. Realizing that Sean wasn't going to go down easy and the cops were on the way, they roared off, leaving their dead friend behind. Sean watched them race down the street. He could hear sirens in the distance. He came up with a quick plan. Whether it was good or not would remain to be seen. He pulled the dead gang member off of the street and placed him in the driver's seat. He took out his wallet, removed the cash and tossed the wallet on the sidewalk. Lastly, he pushed the cigarette lighter in the Jeep and then tossed it in the gasoline leaking from the Jeep. Instantly, the Jeep was engulfed in flames. Sean took off running down the street. He stopped next to a parked silver Honda Accord. He looked around and then smashed the driver's side window. Sean hotwired the Honda and was speeding towards Melrose in less than 20 seconds. Police cars and emergency vehicles flew past him heading for his burning Jeep.

Sean knew where the intersection of Melrose and Highland was and weaved in and out of traffic, doing everything he could to get there. About a quarter of a mile in front of him he could see multiple police cars and an ambulance. He slowed as he approached the scene, scanning the area for any sign of Nat and praying it wasn't her. As he got closer, he saw the BMW motorcycle in a heap behind a sedan. He slowed to a crawl as he passed. Sheriff's deputies, LAPD and the EMTs were standing next to a figure on the pavement draped in a white sheet. Sean lost it. He floored the Honda and left the scene with tears running down his face. He gripped the wheel of the Honda, leaving the impressions of his fingers in the leather. He felt rage taking over his entire body and his anger was now looking for an outlet. Sean was going to deliver of the pain and rage he was feeling to all of the 70's. They would receive no quarter.

With everyone believing he was dead, he'd have plenty of time and the freedom to hunt down every last 70 and kill them as violently as possible.

## 38
## Port of Los Angeles

Sean parked the car a few blocks from his apartment and covered the distance in a near sprint. He raced up the stairs to his apartment, trying to make sure no one saw him. He always had a "go-bag". He picked the bag up off of the floor of the closet, emptied his safe, making sure to grab his remaining passports and cash. Lastly, he carefully placed the picture of Michelle in his bag. He grabbed the Ducati keys and left the apartment, knowing he'd never be back.

Sean gunned the bike through Los Angeles making his way to a storage facility near the Port of Los Angeles. He tapped in a security code, entered and found his unit near the back of facility. It was twilight. The place seemed abandoned, which was the reason chose the location. The alternating colors of the units were nauseating. The few cameras on site had been adjusted by Sean to exclude his storage unit and he'd managed to thwart the camera at the entrance. He opened the unit, flipped on the light and pushed the bike inside. The unit was large at 20'x30'. Sean had outfitted the space anticipating a need to get out of sight. He'd added a small refrigerator, a threadbare rug, cot and a work bench. The item he was most interested in now was the large gun safe in the back of the unit covered by a sheet. He pulled off the sheet, entered the combination for the safe and opened it. He'd stocked it with everything from Glocks and C4 to knives, two Heckler & Koch

G36c ultra short assault rifles and a sniper rifle. He felt like a survival nut when he first set this place up. Sean closed the door and sat down in an old arm chair, he'd found on the street and moved into the space. He was shaking. He couldn't believe they had killed her.

How many times had Natalia avoided being shot or blown up? And at the end of the day it was bunch of thugs in a beat-up van that killed her. Sean had brought this on her. It was his fault. He was now going to make this Flores and the rest of the 70's pay, every last one of them.

Sean opened the safe and pulled out a laptop and a small black notebook. He preferred an Apple, but Mark Phillips had said the Alien model was the most powerful for what Sean wanted to do – hacking. Sean was not an idiot when it came to computers. However, he was not a hacker, but the small notebook in his hand gave him the step-by-step instructions on how to be a damn good one. Sean didn't like the fact that he could be tracked when he logged onto a phone, computer or even if he turned on a TV. The set up on the laptop would make it nearly impossible to find who was about to illegally gain access to the data bases of the LA Country Sheriff's Department, ATF, DEA and FBI. Sean planned on gathering everything he could on the 70s and then wipe them off the face of the Earth.

## 39
## Various Locales

Mrs. Lomax was placing the last dish in the dishwasher and her husband had just returned from taking the trash out. The local news was on television in the living room. It was just background noise.

"More on the impeachment. I'm tired of hearing about it. I heard today that the video might be a fake." Mr. Lomax said, walking into the kitchen and washing his hands.

"You need to stop listening to talk radio. I don't want to believe it either, but I believe that young congressman. What's his name? Mike something?" Mrs. Lomax responded as she folded the dish towel and placed it on the handle of the dishwasher.

The newscaster said something that caught her attention. "Honey, see if you can rewind that," she asked.

Mr. Lomax heard something strange in her voice and went into the living room, picked up the remote and pushed rewind. They both stood in front of the TV. The nightly news began to play. The image of Sean's burned out Jeep and his driver's license photo were on the screen.

"Gangs and gun violence claimed another life this afternoon. Thirty-one-year-old Sean McWilliams was caught in the cross fire between rival gangs. The vehicle he was traveling in was riddled with bullets then burst into flames. Mr. McWilliams was pronounced dead at the scene. In other news, the Oscars are a week away . . . ."

"Oh my god! Oh my god!" Mrs. Lomax began to cry. Her husband put his arms around her. "Why did this happen to him? This breaks my heart."

"I don't know." Mr. Lomax said, hugging her.

"Did he have any family?" She asked.

"I don't think so."

**Langley, Virginia**
**Sametime**

It was Friday night and Mark Phillips was exhausted. He rubbed his eyes and stared at his screen. There were 176 "alerts" that he needed to review. He was too tired. Since David O'Connor had been fired, Phillips' life had become difficult. The interim director didn't care for O'Connor's people and as a result, Phillips was moved to a less than comfortable location in the building and given mainly busy work. He began to throw items into his bag and reached to flip off his monitor. He missed a new alert pop on his screen, alert number 177. It was a short news story regarding a gang related shooting in Los Angeles. Mark flipped off his desk light and went home for the weekend.

**UCLA Medical Center**

A team of nurses and doctors pushed a bloody gurney down the hall, headed towards the OR.

"What's the story with this one?" a doctor asked, looking at an x-ray as he walked next to the gurney.

"Motorcycle wreck. Hit and run." The nurse explained. "They pronounced her dead at the scene, but an EMT found a pulse. She doesn't want to give up."

"Get her into the OR," the doctor ordered, looking at Natalia Molotov's broken body. "Who is she?"

"Jane Doe. No identification and she's not in any system according to the sheriff's department."

"Let's save her and worry about who she is later."

## 40
## Santa Rosa Apartments

Sean had spent three straight days with little or no sleep, pouring over reports from gang taskforces, the FBI and now also Homeland Security and the DEA. Named for a series of streets in East LA, the 70's street gang was a terror. Membership estimates in LA ranged from 100 to 233 members. However, there was a core group of 27 "founders" and their immediate soldiers. The 70's were a conduit for drugs, working with the largest drug cartel in Mexico. They made a fortune selling guns and chopping cars. They also were the worst human traffickers in Southern California. This was the business Sean determined he was going to hit first.

Women coming into LA were handed off to the 70's and housed at the Santa Rosa Apartments on the edge of Compton. They were from all over the world but primarily China and Central America. From there, they were sold off. Sean spent a couple of days watching the building and scouting the area. The whole operation made Sean sick to his stomach. He determined that there were eight to 10 men in the building and more than 30 women. The men seemed to live in the two-story apartment building, abusing the women whenever they pleased.

Alejandro Suarez was the human trafficking point person for the 70s. He was in his early 30's and had been in and out of prison since his teens. He was a brutal and cruel man. Sean studied his "sheet" and watched him at the apartment building. He didn't stay there but checked on his business at least once a day. Sean hated him.

He learned that Homeland Security was also monitoring the building and the gang, but not doing a good job. They didn't seem to be anywhere close to putting a stop to what was going on. Sean however, was ready to move on them.

The Suarez was arrogant and easy to predict. Sean made the arrangements he needed to clean out the apartment and assassinate Suarez.

He stood in his storage unit doing an inventory. He was dressed almost identically as he was when he jumped into Iceland – minus the parachute. His red Ducati was now painted matte black. He hated the DIY paint job, but the red simply stood out too much. At a little after 2AM, Sean left the storage facility and rode the 30 minutes to the apartment complex. He arrived without incident and parked the bike behind a dumpster in an alley near the apartment. Staying in the shadows, he made his way through the alley. A random dog or two barked, but Sean was otherwise undetected. He pulled a damaged portion of fence to the side and entered the lot behind the apartment. The lot was littered with old tires and trash. Large stands of grass grew randomly in the dusty lot. Sean pulled on a pair of night vision goggles and watched the building. A lone man walked around the building once and then sat down on the stairs leading to the second floor. He lit up a joint and stared at his phone. Sean quickly covered the 30 yards between the fence to the side of the apartment. He stopped by the power box and pulled the main circuit breaker, killing the power to the entire building. The joint smoking guard noticed that the power had gone out and got up from his perch. He took two steps only to be met with a suppressed round to the head. He fell backwards, hitting the concrete steps. Sean grabbed his t-shirt and sat him up against the wall. Sean opened the door to the first floor and looked inside. There was a pitch-black hallway with approximately 12 apartments on each side. Sean knew only half were occupied. The women were kept upstairs with just one guard and he was now dead on the stairs. He pulled out a concussion grenade, knowing that as soon as it went off the men in the apartment would come pouring out of the rooms. Sean threw the grenade down the hall and pulled his head back outside. The grenade went off, waking the men and partially filling the hall with smoke. Sean entered the hall with his suppressed Glock ready to inflict as many casualties as possible. Sean picked the 70's off easily as they ran into the hall. The massacre lasted less than eight seconds. Sean went to each room to make sure they were clear and then proceeded back to the door. He raced up the stairs to check on the women. What he found made him sick. Suarez and his men had removed the doors to the rooms and replaced them with bars. For all intents and purposes, it was a prison. As Sean made his way down the hall, the women watched him from behind the bars. He knew he looked terrifying. They didn't say a word. Sean reached the end of the hall. There was a room packed with eight Chinese women. In Mandarin Chinese, Sean told them help was on the way and that they would be ok.

Sean left the second floor, picked up the guard's cell phone and sprinted across the back lot to the fence. He again stayed in the shadows, reaching the bike in a few seconds. He sat on the bike and dialed 911.

"911. What's your emergency?"

"There are 11 dead men at the Santa Rosa Apartments," he said slowly in Mandarin.

"Sir? Sir? I don't understand you."

"Yes?" Sean responded and then repeated himself in broken English.

"Are you injured?"

"There are 30 women being held there on the second floor and need help," Sean added in Mandarin.

"Sir? Are you OK? I'm dispatching units to your location."

Sean tossed the phone into a dumpster in the alley and cautiously rode through the alley and onto the street. He was only on the road for a few minutes before pulling into another alley behind a four-story office building. Sean hid the bike and got off. He jumped and pulled down the building's fire escape, climbed to the roof and walked to the edge. From the building, he had an unobstructed view of the Santa Rosa Apartments. He looked at his watch. Less than 20 minutes had passed. Sean walked over to an HVAC vent and removed the screen. Behind it was a backpack containing a Remington 7.62x51mm NATO/.308 Winchester bolt-action breakdown sniper rifle. He picked up the pack and moved back to the edge of the building. He assembled the rifle and took out a pair of binoculars and scanned the front of the apartment building. Sean knew the street would soon be covered with law enforcement. That's not who he was waiting for. He knew Alejandro Suarez would show up soon.

Sean patiently waited for two hours and was beginning to worry that sunrise would ruin his plans. A little after 5AM, a red pickup made its way down the street. Sean focused on it with the binoculars and then with the scope on the rifle. It was Suarez. The truck slowed about a block from the apartments. The police had cordoned off the area surrounding the apartment.

"Come on. Get out of the truck," Sean said to himself, focusing on the image of the driver through the scope. He didn't have a clean shot with Suarez in the pick-up. Suarez was a little farther way than he'd planned, but he was confident he could take him out. The taillights came on and the truck stopped. Sean adjusted the scope slightly. Three men got out of the truck but not the driver. None of them were Suarez. The three men walked towards the apartment. Sean remained focused on the driver. One of the men turned and waved to the driver.  Sean watched the driver's side door open and a large man put his foot down and get out of the truck.  It was Suarez.  The shot was now over 1,000 meters.  Sean slowed his breathing and squeezed the trigger.  The shot was true and ripped through Suarez's head, breaking the driver's side window in the process and sending bone and brain fragments across the front quarter panel.

Sean pulled the rifle back from the edge of the roof and disassembled the weapon, returning it to the backpack. He left the roof, got on the Ducati, put on his helmet and a black jacket and left the area.

## 41
## Georgetown

"Shit. Shit," Mark Phillips mumbled to himself as he drove to Georgetown from Langley. "I can't believe I missed this." Phillips navigated the Georgetown streets, finally finding a parking spot. He jogged two blocks to a brownstone. Gone was the normal security detail. Phillips walked up to the front door and rang the bell. After several moments, David O'Connor answered.

"Ah, Mark! What a nice surprise. I was expecting more irritated people from the DOJ," O'Connor said.

"May I come in, sir?"

"Of course. Of course," O'Connor said, opening the door for Phillips to enter. O'Connor knew something was wrong.

"I have bad news." Phillips said, fumbling with his bag. His hands were shaking. "I'm late on bringing this to you. I'm sorry. I feel awful."

"Mark, calm down. What is it?"

"Sean is dead."

"What?" David O'Connor placed his hand on a table to steady himself. He'd been close with Sean and felt responsible for him. In addition, several years ago, Sean had volunteered to protect his grandson, putting his life on the line in the process. Sean was more than just an agency asset.

"I'm sorry. I missed the alert."

"Mark. Slowdown. Give me the details."

"I received a news report of a gang related shooting in Los Angeles. The police identified the body. It's Sean." Phillips handed O'Connor the police report, complete with Sean's falsified California driver's license. O'Connor scanned the report.

"Says the body was burned in a car fire triggered by gun fire." O'Connor said, looking up at Phillips.

"They found his wallet and ID on the sidewalk." Phillips added.

The former CIA Director took a few steps towards the living room of his house and turned. "Mark, we're going to Los Angeles."

"You don't think he's dead, do you?"

"I want to be certain."

"I have not reached out to the Molotovs," Phillips added.

"Good. Don't. I'll handle that." O'Connor walked down the hall and began to climb the stairs. "Mark, we leave this morning."

"Mr. O'Connor, I have to be back at Langley."

David O'Connor turned on the stairs and looked at Mark Phillips. "But, do you really? Hmmm?"

Mark Phillips thought about it for a split second. "I really don't."

"Good. Wait right there. You can drive us to Dulles."

"Yes sir."

## 42
## Sean's storage unit
## Los Angeles

Sean used a baby wipe to remove the face paint. He removed all of the weapons and placed them carefully on the work bench. He sat down and took a Gatorade from the mini fridge adjacent to his beat-up arm chair. He took a long drink and leaned his head back, looking at the ceiling. He no longer cared about the moral dilemma of mass murder. He'd stopped caring long ago after he'd learned what the CIA had programmed him to do. These people, the 70's, took something from him. Something he could never replace. They were torturing people. Stealing them from their homes. No one was even trying to stop them, so he would. They needed to be punished.

His reflection period behind him, Sean cleaned each weapon and placed everything back in the gun safe. He finished the Gatorade, stripped down and fell asleep on the cot.

Sean woke up after several hours and realized that he really needed a shower. He threw some clothes into a backpack, locked and left the storage unit. He figured he could slip into a 24-Hour Fitness without being noticed to shower and shave. If he was forced, he'd get a seven-day trial membership. Sean walked into the gym a little after 5PM. The gym's peak period. He got his shower and left without issue. He headed straight for Denny's. He found a table in the back of the restaurant, ordered and pulled out an iPad. He began reviewing videos the ATF had shot a couple of years ago. The videos were mostly of the gang sitting in front of a carwash talking. However, one caught Sean's attention. It was of a funeral. What was interesting was that after the graveside service, wives, family and children left, leaving only the gang at the grave. They passed around a bottle of some sort and tossed the empty bottle into the grave.

"I've got you," Sean said to himself. No kids and no women would be hurt, just the men that killed Nat.

Shooting Suarez now was a strong strategic move. Sean devised a plan to kill as many of the 70's as possible. A funeral or wake for Suarez made for the perfect gathering. He began researching every funeral home in the area looking for a notification. He couldn't find anything and realized that the police had probably not released his body. This gave him time to prep. Sean began researching drones. He needed one powerful and large enough to carry 10 pounds of explosives and ball bearings. He'd figure out how to fly it.

Sean's dinner arrived. He slipped the iPad back into his backpack, thanked the server and dug into his pancakes.

## 43
## LA County Sheriff's Department Gang Task Force

"He was speaking Chinese?" the deputy, Michael Daniels asked, flipping through papers on the group's conference room table.

"Yeah," another deputy, Debbie Torres, answered, re-reading the report. "The FBI is going to be here in about 45 minutes. They might be able to provide some insight."

A third deputy, Max Shepard, was leaning on the windowsill listening. He was a little rougher around the edges than the other two. "This guy is ex-military with an axe to grind. This isn't gang related, other than he wants the 70's dead."

"Max, why do you say that?" Torres asked, turning to look at him.

"How many dead?" Shepard asked.

"Twelve." Torres answered.

"How many shots?"

"Eleven in the apartment. Plus, the shot that killed Suarez." Torres responded.

"Doesn't seem like your typical gang hit. The guy didn't come in there spraying automatic fire. No, this guy was quiet and efficient."

"So, he's Chinese army?" Daniels asked. "The rest of the team thinks it's the Chinese moving in on the 70's turf."

"They are wrong. I doubt the guy is even Chinese. It's a distraction."

"Maybe," Torres answered.

"How far was the shot that killed Suarez?" Shepard asked.

"1021 meters." Daniels answered. "You're an ex-Marine sniper. Could you make that shot?"

Shepard shook his head "no" walked across the room and poured himself more coffee. "There's not many people in the world that can make that shot from that distance. A head shot. At night. And a windy night to boot."

"Well, whoever he is, he's a ghost. Nothing on any traffic camera. We also checked out the cameras in nearby businesses, hoping we'd pick something up. Nothing." Daniels added.

"I doubt this guy will slip up. Let's hope he's done and has moved on," Shepard said, stirring his coffee and sitting down at the conference room table. "He killed some people that are the absolute scum of the earth. I won't miss them."

"We still have a job to do, Max," Torres said, slightly irritated.

"I know we do. Get off your high horse. I'm just afraid of what we're going to find."

## 44
## 435,126
## East LA

Sean stepped off of the bus in front of A+ Autos. He walked down row after row of used cars. He could feel the salesman close behind him.

"Anything in particular you're looking for?" the salesman asked. Sean stopped in front of a beat-up Mazda pickup. He peered into the window. The seats were torn and most of the body panels were rusted.

"I think I like this one," Sean said, patting the roof of the truck.

The salesman adjusted his plaid tie. "You sure?"

"It runs right?" Sean asked, now skeptical of the man, the lot and the truck.

"Yes it does! We ran it through a 50-point inspection." The salesman then waved at the other end of the lot. "It's just that there are better vehicles here."

"I want this one," Sean said confidently. "How much is it?"

"$900."

"Sold," Sean answered. The salesman shook Sean's hand.

"I'm Frank. You are?"

Sean smiled. "Joe. Joe Ippolito."

"Joe, if you'll follow me, we'll get the paperwork going."

"Frank. Can we avoid the paperwork?" Sean asked.

Frank, the salesman, looked at Sean cautiously. "Sir, we have to write this up."

"$2,000. That's $900 for the truck. $1,100 for you."

Frank looked around the lot, expecting the police to swoop down. Nothing happened. He kicked the gravel under his feet. "You have cash?"

"Only cash," Sean answered.

"Wait right here." Sean watched Frank walk across the lot to a small trailer. Sean leaned against the truck. Traffic whizzed by in front of the car lot. The red, white and blue pennant flags strung from the light poles flapped in the breeze. Frank emerged from the trailer with a set of keys in his hand and a license plate.

"Set of keys and a set of plates."

Sean handed him a wad of cash and took the keys and plates.

"Joe, please don't come back here again," Frank said, trying to give Sean a hard look.

"Don't worry. You'll never see me again."

The truck started up on the third try and Sean left the lot.

Sean had located a hobby shop in Corona that carried the drone he was looking for. The drive to Corona was excruciating in the Mazda. He preferred his bike, but there was no way he could transport the drone with the Ducati. In traffic, it took two hours to make the drive. Sean pulled up to Corona RC and parked on the side of the building. The store closed in 10 minutes, but Sean took his time approaching the store. He didn't see any cameras. For once, his slovenly appearance was going to pay dividends. His hair was long and he had a nasty looking beard. He looked the part of a surfer, which he was about to play up. Sean entered the store as the owner was approaching the door to lock it.

"Can I help you? I'm Skip," a short, heavy set man said as Sean entered.

"Yeah, hi Skip. I called earlier about the Yuneec Tornado," Sean said, looking around the store for cameras. He didn't see any.

"Yes! You're Mike, right?" Skip asked, getting excited about a big sale.

"Right. You have it in stock still?" Sean said, walking to the counter. The walls were covered with boxes of remote-controlled cars and drone kits. The clear counter in front of Sean was filled with parts for all sorts of remote-control vehicles: replacement wheels, blades and more gears than Sean could count. The whole place smelled like 3-in-1 oil.

"Yeah. It's right here." Skip walked to the backroom and returned with a large box. "Not many people want to buy this thing given the cost, most want to just look at it."

"My girlfriend is a competitive surfer. She's making a video to pick up new sponsors. We need this. She's really amazing."

Skip leaned on the box. "That's really cool. You're getting the perfect drone to film surfing. You know this thing has a 2-kilometer range and can carry nearly 10 pounds?"

"Yeah, it's perfect," Sean said, reaching into his pocket. "Cash ok?"

"That works." Skip said, happy to make such a huge sale. "Mike, you have made my month."

Sean handed Skip $2,700 in cash and left the store. The drive back to the storage unit was just as rough as the drive to Corona. The odometer on the Mazda read 435,126. Based on the truck's performance, Sean was confident the reading had not been tampered with. However, he was beginning to wonder if the truck would run long enough for him to complete his attack on the 70's. In the back of his mind, part of him was telling him to stop, but that voice was drowned out by another angrier voice telling him that he needed to send these men straight to hell.

Sean spent the rest of the night and early hours of the next day studying the drone. By mid-morning, Sean was ready to test it. He headed out to the beach and took it for a test flight. It was surprisingly easy to operate, and the attached camera was perfect. He was able to maneuver the drone with only the image on the drone's tablet. Satisfied, he returned the drone to the storage unit. He locked up the unit and got on his bike and headed to 24 Hour Fitness for a shower and then over to the barber. The long hair and beard needed to go. He was going to do a little surveillance later in the day.

Cleaned up and now dressed up, Sean parked the Mazda at long term parking facility near LAX. He got on a bus outside of the parking lot and took it to a light rail station. He hopped on the Gold Line to East LA. Sean had on a navy blazer, a white shirt and tan pants. His backpack was thrown over his shoulder. His hair was nearly all buzzed off and he was clean shaven. He looked like a Jehovah's Witness. He walked three blocks from the station to a Roscoe's Chicken and Waffles. He got a seat by the window which gave him a clear view of the carwash across the street. In the car wash's lot and on the street in front were nearly 20 members of the 70's street gang. Sean took his time with the menu while flipping through images on his iPad. He had every mugshot taken of the gang in the last 15 years in addition to the pictures federal and local law enforcement had taken. By the time the chicken and waffles arrived, Sean had identified 90% of the men across the street. He was looking for the men who drove the vehicle that killed Nat. He thought it was a van but wasn't quite sure. He was also looking for Roberto Flores, the man who gave the order to kill her. Sean ate his waffles and watched.

A little less than a mile away, a late model pick-up with a LA County Sheriff decal on the driver's side door was heading for the car wash.

"Max, you sure this is a good idea?" Deputy Torres asked, looking out the passenger side window.

"Yeah. I want to see if these guys are spooked." Shepard adjusted the rear-view mirror as he spoke. "Plus, they might lead us to our guy."

"Our guy?"

"Yeah. The guy that killed all those people. Don't get me wrong, I'm not losing sleep over those guys getting smoked."

"Well, let's call him "your" guy. The rest of us think it's another gang."

Shepard slowed the truck as they approached the car wash and pulled into the parking lot. From across the street, Sean was watching. The two deputies got out of the truck and started walking to the entrance of the car wash. Sean noticed the way the male deputy walked and handled the M4 he slung over his shoulder when he exited the truck. He was a little over 6' tall, with short spiked blonde hair and a dirty beard. Sean knew he was ex-military - probably a Marine. His partner was a Hispanic woman of above average height. She kept her hand on the Glock as she followed her partner.

"What the fuck do you want?" a man said, leaning on a late model Cadillac. The rest of the men were starting to form a semi-circle around the two deputies. Sean watched, sipping his iced tea. His thoughts now turned to the deputies. Could he cover the distance from Roscoe's to the car wash if things went south for the deputies? He took another bite of waffle, eyes glued to the car wash.

"I'm here to talk to Flores," Max Shepard said with an edge. "Go get him."

"He's not here." the man said and then spit at Shepard's feet. Shepard removed his sunglasses and looked at the spit on the ground.

"Go get him now, or I'm going slam your punk ass on the ground and mop that spit up with your fucking face." Shepard said with a deadly tone. The man stared at the deputy for a split second and then nodded to a man behind the two deputies. A few moments later, Roberto Flores appeared. Across the street, Sean shot up straight in his seat.

"What do you want deputy?" Flores said, walking towards Shepard and Torres. The gang began to dissipate, leaving a clear view of the two deputies and Flores.

"You guys had a little trouble the other night," Shepard said, looking around the lot.

"I don't know anything about it. I run a car wash," Flores answered.

"Sure, you do," Shepard said, putting his sunglasses on. "So, no one has been muscling you?"

Flores laughed. "No. No one is bothering me officer. Thank you for checking."

"It's 'deputy'. Let me be more specific. Any run-ins with anyone that might want you dead?"

"No," Flores answered.

"Well, I've been paying attention and I've been keeping score. It sure as shit looks like you're in someone's crosshairs and you're losing." Shepard rolled his shoulders. "If I was a betting man, I'd wager that you're headed for a fight you can't win. The sad thing is, you don't even know it or where it's coming from."

"Get the fuck off my lot," Flores shouted at Shepard.

"I'm leaving. Just remember, I tried to help you." The two deputies got back in their truck.

"Max, he doesn't have a clue," Torres said.

"Nope." Shepard looked both ways to pullout, but Roscoe's caught his eye. "You feel like snack?"

"A snack? At Roscoe's? Let's just call it dinner, ok Max?"

Shepard laughed, drove across the street and found a parking spot. As they approached the restaurant, a tall, fit man held the door open for them.

"Have a great meal guys," Sean said, as the deputies passed.

"Thanks," Max Shepard said, walking past Sean.

Sean got into a waiting cab and left, knowing he'd return to the car wash and that Nat's killers would be there sooner or later.

## 45
## LA County Morgue

David O'Connor and Mark Phillips entered the dreary LA County Morgue and walked up to a reception desk. A LA County Sheriff's deputy was behind the desk.

'May I help you?"

"We're here to identify a body." Mark Phillips answered.

"Which one? We've got a lot." The woman replied with a less than enthusiastic tone.

"Sean McWilliams."

"And who are you?" the deputy asked.

"Family." Phillips replied.

"IDs."

David O'Connor and Mark Phillips handed over their driver's licenses. The deputy logged their names.

"Wait over there." the deputy pointed at two rows of chairs. O'Connor and Phillips sat down. A local news cast was playing on an ancient TV mounted on the wall. The sound was off and there was footage of an apartment building surrounded by police. Bodies were being removed from the building. The super read, "Gang War Erupts."

A man in a white lab coat entered the waiting room. He looked at the paper in his hand. "Mr. O'Connor. Mr. Phillips. I'm the assistant medical examiner. I'm sorry, but I'm afraid there's not much to identify. The body was burned beyond recognition. Mr. McWilliams was identified based on his ID being found near the crime scene."

"Nonetheless, we'd like to take a look. For closure," O'Connor explained. "We also want to coordinate burial."

"Fine," the examiner said, exasperated. He was overworked and underpaid. "Follow me."

The examiner showed O'Connor and Phillips into a large room with a bank of stainless-steel doors on one side. The examiner stopped midway through the room, opened a door and pulled out a shelf. A white sheet covered a completely burned body.

"Not much to identify. Sorry. I'll be over here." The examiner walked away. O'Connor and Phillips stared down at the body, focusing on the right shoulder. They looked at each other.

"We've seen enough," O'Connor said, walking towards the door. "Thank you for your time."

Phillips and O'Connor didn't speak until they got into their rental car.

"That wasn't Sean. The collar bone on that man had never been broken. Sean's child hood break never healed correctly. We'd be able to see that." Phillips said, starting the car.

"No. No it wasn't Sean. So, where is he? And what is he doing?" O'Connor replied.

## 46
## East Los Angeles

Sean spent the day watching the car wash from the roof of a nearby building. The same gang members from the day before lingered for most of the day. Sean ate fried chicken and drank from a gallon jug of water. A light blue Ford van appeared and entered the lot just after 4PM. Sean pulled out binoculars and focused on the front of the van. There was a dent in the front right bumper and the grill was partially smashed. Sean felt he had found the vehicle that killed Nat. Roberto Flores walked out from the car wash bay. Sean watched to see who got out. Flores leaned into the van and spoke to the men inside for several minutes. They never got out. Sean was already climbing down from the roof. He pulled on a black motorcycle helmet and sat on the bike in an alley, watching the car wash. After a few minutes, the van left the car wash and passed by Sean. He pulled into traffic and followed the men in the van. They made several stops, clearly collecting money for Flores. Protection money. Drug money. Sean had no idea and he didn't care.

Around 9PM the van pulled into a lot populated by several food trucks. The three men in the van stopped by each truck and picked up a small bag. More protection money. Two men sat down at a picnic table while the third ordered food from one of the trucks. He returned to the table with a tray full of food. They were laughing and generally not paying attention. Sean was dressed in jeans, a black motorcycle jacket and boots. He got off the bike and examined the front of the van. He could tell there had been an impact. He approached the three. Sean left the black motorcycle helmet on with the visor down. He stood at the end of the table for a moment before they noticed him.

"Who the fuck are you?" one of them said to Sean, leaning back and glaring at him. Sean didn't speak. He looked each of them up and down.

"You talk?" the same man shouted at Sean. Sean didn't react. "You know what? Get the fuck out of here!"

"Did you hit a woman on a bike a week or so ago?" Sean asked, finally speaking. His helmet was still on with visor still down.

"What? What did you say?" a second man said, getting to his feet.

"Your van over there has a dent in the bumper and a damaged grill. Looks like you had an accident."

"Who the fuck are you?"

"I'm looking for the men who killed my friend." Sean said with a menacing tone.

There was a long silence as the men sized up Sean. One started to reach behind his back. Probably for a weapon. Sean didn't really care at this point. He'd found the men that had killed Nat. The three 70's sitting at the picnic table didn't have a chance. Sean put a bullet in each of their heads before they could react. He found the shell casings and placed them in his pocket. He walked across the parking lot, calmly got on his bike and rode off. There weren't any cameras in the food truck lot, but there were plenty of witnesses. However, these were witnesses that were sick and tired of paying protection.

Max Shepard showed up at the food truck lot 30 minutes after Sean had left. Torres and Daniels were already there. Caution tape surrounded the lot. Shepard stood at the end of the table and studied the scene. The three men had not yet been moved. The gravel around the table had turned a nasty shade of red.

"Three head shots," Torres said, walking up and standing next to Shepard. "I don't think these guys had a chance. Oh, and another thing, he picked up the casings."

"No, they didn't have a chance. This is the same guy that cleaned out the apartment building. Who else goes to the trouble to pick up evidence?" Shepard said.

"You don't know it's the same guy," Torres challenged. "Look, these three were picking up collections. They had just gotten finished shaking down the food trucks. I say the apartment killing are unrelated. These guys were getting robbed and the killer got spooked before rifling through the van."

"So, your robber didn't take anything? Most robbers take something." Shepard replied, with an irritated look.

"He got spooked," Torres said, defending her theory.

Shepard stood over one of the bodies. It had fallen awkwardly, but the man's face was looking up at the sky. "You see that Torres?"

"Yeah."

"Men committing stick ups don't shoot like this. They fire in a panic. Some are lucky to hit anything. This guy shoots exactly like the shooter from the apartment." Shepard looked around. "Any witnesses?"

"One," Torres answered.

"All this and just one?"

"These three were not popular." Deputy Daniels led an older woman over to Shepard. She was in her 50's and ran the hot dog truck. She had on a mustard stained white apron, jeans and a pair of Crocs.

"Max, this is Mrs. Johnson," Daniels said, introducing her.

"Mrs. Johnson, I'm Deputy Shepard. What did you see?"

"First, you people should have been here to keep these three from robbing me for the last three years!"

"What did you see?" Shepard said, ignoring her.

"Second, I'm glad they're dead," she added.

"I get it. They're pieces of shit. What happened?"

"Guy walks up, talks to them for less than a minute and then shoots them dead." Mrs. Johnson said, without any remorse.

"You see his face?" Shepard asked.

"As I told the other deputy, he was wearing a motorcycle helmet with the visor down. He never took it off."

"Not even the visor?"

"No. He shot them, picked something off the ground, got on his bike and left."

"Anything else?"

"Yeah, before he shot them, he stopped and looked at the van."

"The van?" Shepard asked again.

"Deputy, are you deaf? Yes, the van."

## No Shortcut Home

Shepard turned and studied the van, momentarily forgetting about Mrs. Johnson.

"Can I go?" Mrs. Johnson asked, irritated, but silently thrilled that she no longer needed to pay protection. Shepard half waved and walked over to the van. Deputy Daniels followed him.

"You look this thing over?" Shepard asked.

"Yeah. Couple bags of cash. Some guns. Nothing special. The shooter didn't take anything."

Shepard walked around the van several times. He stood in front of the vehicle, expecting something to pop out at him. "It's just a beat-up van."

"Yup. A piece of crap van." Deputy Daniels added, agreeing with Shepard.

## 47
## LAX Hilton Lobby

"Are you going to have to testify?" Mark Phillips asked David O'Connor, pointing to a copy of *The Los Angeles Times*. "Impeachment Looming" was the banner headline on the front page.

"I certainly hope not," O'Connor answered. He picked up the paper and turned to a story in the local section. The headline read, "Three Dead in Food Truck Gangland Murder."

"You see this story, Mark?" O'Connor answered.

Phillips picked up the paper and read the story. "Same gang as the apartment murders."

"Yes. Same gang. Lone gunman in a motorcycle helmet. No leads."

"So, you think this is Sean? Why would he go after them?" Phillips asked.

"Do they know who shot up the Jeep where the ID was found?"

"No," Phillips answered.

"Heaven help these people if it is Sean." O'Connor replied, taking a sip of coffee.

"You really think he'd do this kind of thing?"

"Mark, I think you've been read into most of Sean's background. He's a good man, but after what he went through, some of the more primal emotions buried deep in his subconscious can come to the forefront, making Sean an extremely calculating and ruthless personality. What was done to him changed him. He was manipulated by drawing on his fear of loss. Pushing him and leveraging this element of his psyche, turned him into a brutal killer. It was awful and it took place right under our noses. You saw what he did to the North Koreans."

"Yeah, I did," Phillips said, remembering Sean's covert fight with elements of North Korea's intelligence service. "What would have triggered him?"

"Something happened. Something terrible. I don't think he'll stop until he's killed every last one of these people." O'Connor said, placing his coffee cup on the table. "Mark, see if we can determine where the deputy in charge of the sheriff's department gang task force stands with investigation."

"Max Shepard."

"Yes. You'll need to handle this carefully and approach it with caution. Gather what you can on this mess and then get in front of Deputy Shepard and his task force. Find out where his head is on this. Your Homeland contact will be the way in. I think Shepard is probably close to figuring this out."

"Why do you say that?"

"I made a couple calls. I talked to his former C.O. and a contact here in LA. He's an ex-Marine with an issue with authority. He's not one to follow along and he's exceptionally intelligent. If something stinks, he's going to figure out where the smell is coming from."

"Sounds like your kind of guy," Phillips said. "I pray it's not Sean."

"We are assuming it's Sean. For all we know, he's on an island somewhere, sitting under an umbrella with a beer in his hand," O'Connor said optimistically.

## 48
## Boom

Sean carefully placed a 3"x1" piece of C4 explosive into a ½ gallon glass jar, making sure it was secured in exactly the middle of the jar. Wires came out of the C4 and were draped over the edge of the jar. Sean carefully filled the jar with a mix of ball bearings and screws. He fed the wires through a small hole in the jar's lid and screwed on the lid. He attached the wires to a cell phone that he taped to the outside of the jar. He sat back and reviewed his work. The drone was already prepped to carry the jar. Sean didn't want to push the max payload of the drone and made sure its weight came in a full pound below the 10-pound max of the drone. It was 4AM. He sat in his beat-up chair, turned out the light and got some sleep. The Suarez funeral was at 11AM. He needed a couple hours of sleep.

Sean parked the Mazda pick-up in the parking lot of a multi-use sports complex. He had on jeans and a sweatshirt. A baseball cap obscured his face. There were a handful of people jogging on the trails that zig zagged through the complex. Thankfully, it was mid-morning on a Thursday and there were not any athletic leagues using the fields. Sean pulled off the moving pads that covered the drone, picked it up and placed it on the ground several yards from the truck. He pushed a couple of buttons on the tablet that controlled the drone. It took off with no effort and shot straight up, reaching 200 feet in the air. Sean then directed the drone towards the cemetery, which was a little more than a quarter of a mile away. On the tablet's display, he could see the cemetery and the funeral service from the drone's on-board camera. He had the drone hover as he watched the service. There were approximately, 20 members of the 70's at the grave site. He couldn't tell if Flores was there. He was the primary target. There were no children there, but 15 or more women. Sean looked at the flight time timer. He had 13 minutes of flight time left. He'd abort before hurting any of the women. Sean stood in the field, staring at the tablet. With eight minutes left, the women and priest began to leave the grave site. They took their time walking down a small hill to the cars. The cars were protected by a line of old oak trees and a stone wall. Sean had calculated the blast radius and was somewhat confident that there would be no collateral damage. Somewhat confident. Not 100 percent.

The 70's were behaving exactly as they had in the ATF surveillance videos, the men gathered closer to the grave of Alejandro Suarez and pulled out a bottle. Each took turns drinking out of the bottle and passing it to the next man. There was now three minutes of flight time left. Sean maneuvered the drone closer to the grave site, maintaining the drone's altitude at 200 feet. The gang didn't notice the hum of the drone. Someone else did.

"What the hell is that?" Deputy Max Shepard said from the edge of the cemetery looking at the drone above the 70's. "Hand me those binoculars." Shepard focused on the drone. "Holy shit! Get those people out of there!"

Shepard was too late. Sean commanded the drone to rapidly descend. Some of gang noticed the drone. However, they had no clue what was about to happen. At approximately 10 feet off of the ground Sean detonated the jar, obliterating the drone and sending ball bearings and metal screws into the gang members and everything in a 40-foot radius. The cars containing the women were pelted by very little shrapnel and no one was injured.

"Get ambulances out here now!" Shepard said, running towards the scene.

Sean turned off the tablet and tossed it into a storm drain next to the truck. He jumped into the Mazda and left the parking lot. He drove for an hour without incident, eventually pulling into a salvage yard. He pulled up to a trailer and got out. A man in coveralls came out of the trailer.

"Can I help you?" he asked from the trailer's stairs.

"Yeah, I want to sell this truck for scrap." Sean shouted above the sound of heavy machinery.

The man walked down from the steps and looked at the truck. "What's wrong with it."

"It barely runs. I'm tired of fighting it. What will you give me for it?"

The man looked it over. "Hundred bucks?"

"Deal, but I get to see you crush it."

"You got it. Wait right there." The man entered the trailer and came back with a handful of 20s and handed the cash to Sean. "I'll be back. Get what you need out of it." The man walked around a pile of flattened cars. Sean looked around the lot. There were thousands of cars, flattened and stacked neatly in rows. He turned and saw the same man behind the wheel of a fork lift. He waved for Sean to get out of the way. Sean took a dozen steps back and watched the fork lift impale the old Mazda and lift it off of the ground. The man motioned for Sean to follow him. Sean walked behind the fork lift. The Mazda was deposited on a car crusher. The man jumped down from the fork lift and walked over to a control panel.

"You best get over here with me in case some parts fly off of that thing."

"Sure thing," Sean said, double timing it over behind the control panel. In less than 15 seconds, the Mazda was destroyed.

"Happy?" the man said, removing his heavy gloves.

"Very," Sean responded. He left the salvage yard and walked the half a mile to a bus stop. He waited there for 20 minutes before a bus arrived. He hopped on, took a seat and headed back to the storage unit.

## 49
## Too Much

David O'Connor and Mark Phillips sat in O'Connor's hotel suite with the TV turned to CNN. The attack in the cemetery was now national news. Every network had crews at the scene. The footage was awful. Trees surrounding the grave site were pitted by shrapnel. The drone attack left 17 gang members dead. Thankfully, there were no injuries or casualties among the families that had attended the funeral. The LA County Sheriff's department was combing the scene. White sheets covered the 17 bodies littering the ground.

"Oh my god. This is one of the worst things I have ever seen. What is Sean doing?" Mark Phillips said.

"We can't jump to conclusions." O'Connor studied the image on the screen. "It's clear that whoever executed this attack only wanted to target the gang and not the families. The blast was very precise. We need to keep digging."

"I will. It's that this looks really bad. I pray it's not Sean."

"We both do," O'Connor answered. He was placing papers into a brief case and looking at his phone.

"How long will you be at the U.N.?" Phillips asked.

"Until the peace accord with Iran is finalized. We're fortunate the Europeans stepped in to fix this mess." O'Connor answered, shaking his head.

"What about the Chinese?"

"They are quite angry. However, making sure that video was made public helped. It saved them from having to do it. Sean handing it off to the congressman was stroke of genius." O'Connor headed for the door. "Keep me posted on all of this."

"Yes sir."

Across town, Max Shepard was combing the crime scene looking for anything that would point to the bomb's point of origin. Deputy Torres followed closely behind him.

"Max, have you ever seen anything like this?"

Shepard stared at the scorched earth under his feet. "Yeah, in Iraq. However, this was very precise and done to avoid any unnecessary casualties. This was done by a pro. I hope the rest of you people can now see that this was not done by a rival gang. This guy clearly has been studying the 70's. I wouldn't be surprised if he has access to all the same intel that we do or even more."

"I think you're right," Torres said. "Were you able to see what kind of drone this was?"

"No and it looks like it was completely destroyed in the blast."

"The guy piloting it had to have a line of site," Torres said, grasping for anything she could.

"No. No, he didn't. Some of these drones can be piloted from more than two miles away. He could be sitting on his couch doing this for all we know." Shepard put his hands on his hips and looked around the cemetery. "Flores wasn't here. Neither were his top men. We need to keep a closer eye on him. This guy will be coming for him"

"Protection? For Flores? How many people has he killed and gotten away with it?" Torres asked, a little dismayed.

"You're missing the point. Flores is the bait. If we wait, our guy will show himself. I imagine he knows that he missed Flores in this attack."

"Ok. Ok. I'm in your camp on this now. I'll make it happen. What about the Feds? Our phones are ringing off the hook," Torres answered. Max Shepard bent down and picked up a ball bearing. He rolled it around in his hand.

"Let's set up a meeting with them. FBI, ATF, Homeland. I'd like to see what they have to say. The FBI was worthless last time we spoke with them. They might have something now. Maybe. I doubt it, but you never know."

"You got it. I'll let you know when."

"Soon Torres. This guy is way ahead of us and doesn't make mistakes."

Shepard threw the ball bearing on the ground, adjusted the dusty baseball cap on his head and walked down the hill with Torres toward the mass of media that was assembled behind the caution tape.

## 50
## LA County Court House
## Gang Task Force Conference Room

"Mark, this is a huge favor. Don't make me regret it. Homeland would have a fit it they knew what I was doing," Blake Samson said to Mark Phillips as they got on the elevator. Samson pressed 11 and the doors closed. Phillips adjusted his "visitors" badge.

"Nothing to worry about. I think we can help with this, but need to stay under the radar," Phillips answered.

"Don't screw me."

"Calm down. Have I ever let you down?" Phillips answered.

"Yeah, Rose Anderson. Remember her? You introduced us and she turned into a total nut job," Samson said, as the doors opened.

"Come on. You guys were happily married for what? A couple years?"

"Eight months, you ass."

Mark slapped him on the back. "Water under the bridge."

"Whatever."

Samson and Phillips were shown into the conference room. The FBI and ATF were already there. Two LA Country deputies were seated near the head of the table. Mark immediately realized why O'Connor liked Max Shepard. Shepard wasn't sitting at the table. He was leaning on the windowsill with his arms crossed. He had on boots, worn out jeans and a LA County Sheriff's Department t-shirt. His arms were covered with tattoos and he didn't seem to care if they were exposed. He had a skeptical look on his face as he surveyed the group. Phillips and Samson sat down next to Deputy Torres. She kicked off the meeting.

"Thank you for being here. We'd like to loop in other agencies to coordinate efforts to stop the sudden escalation of gang violence. We have . . ."

The FBI cut her off. "Sorry to interrupt. We have solid intelligence that points to the Chinese. The Triads."

"And what's that?" Torres responded, a little miffed that she was cut off.

"The 911 tapes for one. The man who called in the killings at the apartment was Chinese."

Torres shook her head. "He spoke Chinese. We don't know if he was Chinese." She tapped a pencil on the table as she looked at the two men from the FBI. "That's what you're basing this on? The 911 call?"

Mark Phillips cleared his throat. Samson kicked him under the table. Phillips spoke anyway.
"What the FBI is saying makes sense. Over the last 24 months, the Triads have lost significant footholds in western Europe to the Albanian and Russian mobs. They clearly see the drug trade here in Southern California as lucrative and the gangs that control it as easy targets. The Triads run a very structured organization. They are efficient and ruthless. They are betting that they can fill a void here in LA and cultivate a relationship with the Mexican cartels. If they are successful, the drug problems will escalate. However, the gang related violence will subside."

"How?" Deputy Daniels asked, skeptical as the deputies had their own theory.

"It's quite simple, there will be no one left. They will eliminate any rival that opposes them."

"How do you explain the killings?" Torres asked. The room now was hanging on Mark Phillips' every word.

"The Triads recruit from the Chinese military. They often will steal the best from Chinese special forces," Phillips explained.

"Makes sense." The ATF agent said, nodding and taking notes. "They did the same thing in Montreal. Same tactics."

"Who the hell are you?" Max Shepard said from the back of the room. His eyes drilled into Mark Phillips' head.

Phillips stammered. "I'm just an analyst."

"That's not what I asked. Who the hell are you?" Shepard demanded as he came closer to Mark Phillips' end of the table. He stopped and stood behind Deputy Daniels with his arms crossed.

"He's one of our analysts focused on organized crime." Blake Samson answered, trying to maintain Phillips' cover.

"Let him talk. He wouldn't shut up a minute ago."

"My name is Andrew Tate," Phillips answered.

"Mr. Tate. That was really good. However, I don't agree with all of it."

"It's just a theory, Deputy Shepard."

"Sounds like more than that," Shepard replied. Phillips decided to shut up. Thankfully, the ATF team felt the need to talk about Montreal and the spotlight was off of Phillips. The meeting lasted another 30 minutes with the FBI dominating the meeting. They talked a lot but really didn't say anything. Everyone began filing out of the room.

"Mr. Tate. Can you please stay behind?" Shepard asked before Phillips left the room.

Phillips froze. "Yeah sure." He let everyone pass him on the way out the door. Blake Samson stayed as well.

"What are you doing?" Shepard asked Samson.

"You said to stay."

"No, I asked him to stay. You may leave and close the door behind you."

"Asshole." Samson whispered under his breath.

"What was that?" Shepard asked in a mocking tone. Samson slammed the door behind him. Shepard pointed to the seat in front of Phillips. "Have a seat."

"How can I help you Deputy?"

"It's interesting that you think that a member of the military committed these murders."

"It's a theory. That's all."

"No, you presented this as if it was fact. Why?"

"Deputy, I'm guessing you've come to the same conclusion. All of the killings were done with a high level of planning and execution. Not something a typical gang banger is capable of."

"I agree Mr. Tate. I agree." Shepard put both hands on the table and leaned closer to Phillips. "However, I don't think he's Chinese."

"Oh? And you base this on what?" Phillips challenged.

"My gut."

Mark Phillips got up from the table. "Well, Deputy, when you have more than that, please call us. Everything we have is pointing towards the Triads." Phillips opened the door. "Good day Deputy."

Blake Samson was standing by the elevator. They both got on.

"What the hell? Mark, you were supposed to keep your mouth shut."

Mark Phillips watched the numbers on the elevator as it descended thinking about what O'Connor's reaction would be.

## 51
## What Set Off Sean

Mark Phillips sat in his hotel room staring at his computer screen. After several minutes, he began furiously typing. Finding out what triggered Sean was so simple. At least it was for him. He got into the databases for the LAPD and sheriff's department and began to research every crime that took place in the city days before and the day that Sean's Jeep was shot to pieces. There was a lot of crime in LA. Phillips combed through the databases for most of the morning. Just before lunch he found something. A hit and run the same day that Sean was attacked. A woman, approximately 25 to 35 years of age, on a BMW motorcycle was hit by a vehicle and thrown from the bike. The vehicle left the scene. She was mistakenly pronounced dead at the scene. An EMT found a faint pulse and she was rushed to UCLA Medical Center and admitted as a Jane Doe. No identification. The motorcycle she was riding didn't have plates. Her fingerprints were not in any database.

Phillips entered the UCLA Medical Center mainframe. Jane Doe was still in intensive care in a coma. He closed his laptop, leaned back in his chair and rubbed his temples. He knew Sean had a thing for bikes and the woman was roughly Sean's age. Could he have known her? Maybe?

Phillips left the room, got in an Uber and headed over to the UCLA Medical Center. He wandered around for a few minutes before asking for

directions to the ICU. Phillips tried to look
inconspicuous but failed. A nurse saw him and
thought he looked lost.

"May I help you sir?" she asked, putting a clipboard
under her arm as she spoke.

"I'm looking for a woman that came in roughly two
weeks ago. A motorcycle accident."

"And you are?"

"Investigating. It was a hit and run I believe."

She looked at him for a moment and finally waved
her clipboard. "Follow me." Phillips followed her
down the hall until she stopped in front of a glass
walled room. Phillips took one look and knew who
it was.

"On my god." he said under his breath. It was
Natalia Molotov. Everything was clear now.

The nurse asked, studying Mark Phillips' face.
"She's barely holding on. She was mistakenly
declared dead at the scene. She's a fighter. The
other nurses think she's some kind of model.
We've been trying to figure out who she is. We've
been looking through fashion magazines to see if
we can find her." The nurse turned and faced him.
"Do you know her?"

"No." Phillips was staring at Natalia Molotov.
There were tubes everywhere. She was in really
bad shape. "No. Sorry. I don't. Thank you for your

help." He left the ICU, dialing his phone as he walked.

"Hello Mark. Have you found anything?" David O'Connor asked, sitting in the office of his Georgetown home. A copy of *The New York Times* and *The Washington Post* were in front of him. Headlines celebrating the signing of peace accords between Iran and the U.S. were adjacent to impeachment developments.

"It's Natalia Molotov. She's in the UCLA Medical Center ICU."

O'Connor slumped in his chair. "What happened?"

"Hit and run. The motorcycle she was on was struck by another vehicle. I'm assuming it was the same gang that attacked Sean. Both incidents happened the same day. She was mistakenly declared dead at the scene."

"And Sean believes she's been killed," O'Connor added. "He doesn't know that she's alive."

"No, it doesn't look like he does. What do you want me to do?" Phillips asked.

"Stay there. Keep digging. I'm going to Pavel's house right now. I'll call Sergei on the way."

"Let me know when you arrive in LA, I'll meet you at the hospital."

"Mark, if this is Sean and now I think it is, we need to find a way to get in touch with him."

"I've been trying. He doesn't want to be found and has gone completely dark. He's not touched any of his off-shore accounts or used any credit card linked to his aliases."

"Figure it out Mark and do it fast," O'Connor said in a tone filled with urgency. "I don't see Pavel and Sergei taking this well."

"Yes sir," Phillips said. He felt a great sadness wash over him. He liked Sean and his heart ached for him. The things that had happened to him were horrific and he'd finally found someone that got him, understood and could deal with his past, only to have her ripped away from him. That being said, Sean had to be stopped. Phillips took an Uber back to his hotel.

## 52
## LA County Sheriff's Department Impound Lot

"Max what are we doing here?" Deputy Torres asked, clearly not wanting to be there.

"I'm looking for that piece of shit van," Shepard said scanning the lot.

"The one from the food truck court?"

"The same," he answered, focused on finding the van. "There it is." Torres followed Shepard to the back of the lot. "There's something here. I know it." He stopped in front of the van and studied the bumper and grill.

"See anything?" Torres asked, mocking him.

"This van collided with something." He got down on one knee and rubbed away some dust from the bumper. "There's a small bit of red paint."

"So?" Torres asked

"So, we're looking for the motive for our guy to go off the rails and systematically kill the 70's."

"I guess he is our guy since every other law enforcement agency is investigating the Triads," Torres said.

Shepard stood up. "They're wrong." He put his hands on his hips and studied the van again as if it was going to start talking and give him the answer.

"Could you please pull a report of every hit and run over the last month?"

"Every single one?" Torres asked, thinking about her workload and now this wild goose chase.

"Yes."

"Well you did say 'please'. I don't think you've used that word in the five years we've worked together."

"Funny."

## 53
## Tip Top Food Store
## 11:13PM

Sean had been following the three 70's all night. They were cruising in a late model Chevy Impala with no particular destination. They were extremely skittish and who could blame them? More than two dozen of their membership had been killed in the last week. Sean sat on his bike across from the Tip Top Food Store and watched them. There were three rows of pumps and the lot was well lit. Sean noticed two sets of cameras focused on the lot. He was hoping the men were going to lead him to Flores. They parked in front of the market and all three entered the store. One headed straight for the men's room and the other two were looking through the reach-in coolers for beer. A red Ford pick-up truck entered the lot and parked next to one of the gas pumps. The driver got out and began pumping gas.

"No. No. No." Sean said out loud. It was an off-duty sheriff's deputy. He had on jeans and a t-shirt with a small star printed on the front pocket of the shirt and "SHERIFF" printed on the back. He didn't see the gang members, but they saw him. The deputy left the truck and headed into the market. Two of the 70's were moving to confront the deputy.

"Hey! Cop! Get the fuck out of here!" one shouted, standing in the entry to the store.

"Guys. I'm just grabbing some food," Deputy Michael Daniels answered, not wanting a confrontation.

"Asshole, you need to do something. Someone is killing us and you're not doing shit," the second 70 shouted.

Daniels recognized a bad situation when he saw one. He stepped backwards to head to his truck. "Alright guys. I get it. I'm leaving."

The 70's were angry and they were going to exact their pound of flesh now. "You know what? Fuck you!" the first man said, reaching around his back to grab a weapon. Sean anticipated what was going down, he flipped the visor down on his helmet and rocketed across the street on the Ducati. However, he didn't get there in time to prevent the deputy from being shot. Daniels took a shot directly to the chest. He fell flat on his back. By this time, Sean was in the lot and had his Glock extended in his left hand. He got off two shots that struck each of the thugs in the chest. They fell to the ground. Sean skidded to a stop and got off the bike. He stood over both men and put a bullet in their heads. He turned his attention to the deputy. The blood was quickly covering his shirt. Sean kneeled down next to the deputy and pulled up his shirt.

"You're going to be ok buddy. You're going to be ok," Sean reassured him. Sean gently lifted the deputy up to look for an exit wound. There wasn't one. Sean could tell it was a sucking chest wound. The lung was punctured. "What's your name?"

# No Shortcut Home

"Daniels."

"Deputy Daniels, you have a sucking chest wound. You're going to be ok. Do you have a first aid kit in your truck?" Sean asked. Daniel's nodded. Sean ran to the truck, found the kit, but also found the radio. He picked it up and called for help.

"This is Deputy Daniels. 10-999! Shots fired! Officer down! 10-999! Assistance needed! Tip Top Food Store. Halsey and 75$^{th}$." He dropped the radio and ran to Daniels. He kneeled down to attend to him. As soon as he opened the kit, a shot ricocheted off the pavement next to them. The third guy. Sean had forgotten about him. Sean pulled the Glock back out, spun and shot the third 70 twice in the chest as he ran out of the store. The man fell on his face in front of the door. Sean immediately turned back to Daniels.

"Ok. This will hurt, but you'll feel better." Sean inserted the needle into the deputy's chest and released the pressure via a valve. "I called it in. Help is coming."

The Korean shop owner ran into the parking lot yelling at Sean. Sean answered back in Korean, "Get me towels. Clean towels." The man was startled to hear Sean speak Korean, but he listened. He ran back into the store and returned with a stack of towels. Sean rolled one up and placed it under Daniel's head. He told the shop owner where to apply the pressure to the entry point. Ambulance sirens were getting closer.

"Deputy, I'm going to stay with you until the ambulance arrives. You're going to be ok, buddy." Sean patted him on the head when he spoke. "You're going to make it. I won't let you die."

Daniels couldn't speak, but gave Sean a thumbs up, looking at his reflection in Sean's visor. The ambulance was the first on the scene. Sean could hear police sirens close behind. The EMTs jumped out of the ambulance.

"He's got a gunshot wound to the chest. No exit wound. Sucking chest wound. He's lost some blood." Sean shouted as he got on the Ducati. The EMTs glanced at Sean as they ran to the deputy. Sean gunned the bike out of the parking lot and sped away from the scene.

Eight sheriff deputies arrived within minutes as well as four LAPD patrol cars. Max Shepard's Dodge pick-up made it nine deputies on site. The EMTs had Daniels on a gurney and were wheeling him to the ambulance.

"He going to be ok?" Shepard asked, walking alongside the gurney. Daniels had an oxygen mask on and was semi-conscious.

"Don't know. Chances are really good. The guy on site took care of the sucking chest wound and stopped the bleeding," an EMT answered as he loaded Daniels into the back of the ambulance.

"The Korean guy?"

"No. Some guy on a bike. He fled the scene when we arrived."

Shepard noticed the three dead men lying on the concrete. "Shit." He shouted at the EMTs "Where are you taking him?"

"UCLA Medical Center."

"Michael! You're going to be ok!" Shepard yelled as the doors to the ambulance closed.

"Max, you're not going to believe this." Torres said, shaking her head and motioning for Shepard to come over. The owner of the store was standing next to one of the gas pumps talking to a deputy.

"Mr. Lee, this is deputy Max Shepard. He heads up the gang task force." Torres said introducing the two.

"Mr. Lee, I'm sorry this happened. Thank you for giving aid to deputy Daniels."

"It was not me. It was a man on a motorcycle,"

Shepard was still skeptical. "What did he do?"

"He stabilized your man. The man who was shot," Lee explained.

"What else?"

"He was watching the store prior to those three attacking the deputy."

"How do you know?" Shepard asked.

"I saw him. He was sitting on a motorcycle across the street. He was watching the three dead men. When he saw that your deputy was in danger, he raced over here."

Shepard ran his hands over his face, put his hands on his hips and looked up at the cameras on the lot. He pointed at the cameras. "These work?"

"They all do. I'm tired of getting robbed," Lee added.

"Can we take a look at the tapes?" Shepard asked.

"Yes! That's why I bought the cameras. The monitors are in the office." Lee lead the deputies into the store but stopped before entering. "One more thing. He spoke Korean."

Shepard made a face. "Korean? Are you sure?"

Mr. Lee pointed at his own face. "Yeah, I'm sure. I'm Korean." He stepped over the body that nearly blocked the entrance and entered the store. The deputies followed.

"So, he's Korean?" Torres asked Shepard.

"No. I still think it's one guy. He may be more of a problem than I thought however."

Mr. Lee unlocked the office and showed Shepard how to operate the cameras and monitors. They watched the three 70's enter the lot and then the store. A couple minutes later Deputy Daniels pulled into the lot and began pumping gas. The deputies were glued to the screen.

They watched in horror as Deputy Michael Daniels was shot point blank. A motorcycle then entered the frame from the right. The rider extended his left hand and shot both 70's.

"Did you see that? Who can shoot like that?" a deputy asked from the back of the office. The video continued rolling. The rider got off the bike, stood over both 70's and shot them in the head.

"Jesus!" Torres blurted out. Shepard looked over his shoulder at her. She stopped talking.

"What's he doing?" a deputy asked. "Does he leave that damn helmet on the whole time?"

"He's examining Daniels. Trying to save him," Shepard answered calmly, knowing that things just got more complicated for him. The rider ran to Daniels' truck. They could see him on the radio. He returned with the first aid kit.

"He called it in. Not Daniels." Torres said. The deputies watched as the rider treated the sucking chest wound. On a second monitor, the third 70 came up behind the rider and Daniels. The rider shot and killed the third man so fast that Shepard rewound it.

"I've never seen anyone move that fast," Torres said. "What's he doing now? Why isn't he leaving?"

Shepard cleared his throat. "He's comforting Michael. He's clearly not going to leave him even it means he's caught." An ambulance entered the lot. The rider stood up and was briefing the EMTs. He then got on his bike and left the lot.

"He never took off that helmet," Torres said.

"He saved Daniel's life" a deputy said from the back of the room.

Shepard spun around in the chair to face the group of deputies and two LAPD officers that had just watched the video. "Yeah. Yeah. He did." Shepard crossed his arms. "He's still a killer and we have a job to do."

One of the LAPD officers blurted out, "Fuck that. He just saved a cop's life and killed some shitty people. Looks like self-defense to me." He elbowed his partner and left the room. Shepard glared at them.

"I can't control those two. I'm going to tell you that we're not letting up on this guy." Shepard said to the group of deputies. They were silent. But they saw it with their own eyes. Sean killed three men that intended to kill a fellow deputy and a friend. He'd saved Daniel's life.

"Got it Max," Someone said from the back. Everyone but Torres left the room. She stood there, arms crossed glaring at Shepard.

"What do we do? This guy saved Daniels. We don't have one clue who he is. Is he white? Black? Chinese? Or, now Korean? And, how do we know that he doesn't just vanish. Hell, he's killed more than 30 of them now." Torres ranted.

Shepard leaned back in his chair. "We're going to catch him." Shepard got up. "Don't ever let anyone hear you speak that way. You're better than that and it's your job to catch this guy. I'm glad you got it off your chest, but never again. Do you understand?"

Torres immediately realized that she'd said too much. "Sorry Max. You're right."

Mr. Lee was now standing in the doorway. Shepard shook his hand. "Thank you for helping our friend. We owe you."

"You're welcome. I hope he's ok."

"Me too. Would you be able to share this video with us? I can send someone down to get it."

"No need. I'll email it to you right now." Mr. Lee said, brushing past the deputies and sitting in the chair in front of the monitors. "Like I said, I don't want to get robbed and I spent extra on this system. What's the email address?"

Torres handed him her card.

"Done. If you need me for anything else. You let me know."

"We will." The deputies turned to leave.

"Oh, Deputy Shepard."

"Yeah."

"I've never seen a bike like the one this guy was on. On the street at least."

Now the deputies were all ears. "What do you mean?"

"It was a Ducati Panigale. I'm pretty sure a V4 R as well."

"So?"

"I've only seen them in magazines. It's a $40,000 bike. There's not a lot of them around. My son has a poster of one on his bedroom wall."

Shepard snapped his fingers. "Awesome." He looked at Torres. "Let's track the bike down."

"On it."

Across town, Sean pulled the Ducati into the storage unit, knowing that he'd probably never ride it again. It was burned. It was way too flashy, and he was stupid to be on it in the first place. He'd bought the bike in cash at an auction and was doubtful it could ever be tracked to him. He placed his helmet on the bike's seat. He was getting tired of living in what was basically a shed. He sat down on his chair and took a beer out of his mini fridge. He sipped the beer and thought about Deputy Daniels and was glad he was there. The gang would have executed him in the parking lot. He looked at the second bike he had in the storage unit. It was the hot Kawasaki Ninja ZX 10RR, covered by a sheet for the time being. It was lime green and one of only 500 produced. Yeah, still flashy. Like the Ducati, it couldn't be traced back to him. Nat said he had a problem with buying bikes. Sean had told her there were worse habits.

He picked up an iPad from the top of the fridge and flipped through the files on Flores. He knew he was going to be tough to find. He'd ride past the carwash in the morning to see if there was any sort of activity. The whole storage unit smelled like a sweaty motorcycle shop. He finished his beer, poured water over his face and wiped the water off with a towel. The water collected and slowly ran towards the drain in the middle of the room. Sean placed a small amount of toothpaste on his toothbrush and paced, while brushing. He spit the toothpaste into the beer bottle and rinsed his mouth out and spit into the beer bottle a second time. He placed the nasty bottle into a trash bag, realizing his life was fueled only by revenge and rage. He was living like a survivalist in the middle of one of the world's largest cities. After securing everything in the gun safe, he sat in his chair, turned off the light and went to sleep.

## 54
## Nat

Max Shepard was sitting at the task force's conference table watching the video from the night before for the 18th time when Deputy Torres walked into the room and slapped a set of papers down on the table. The early morning California sun was pouring through the windows behind Shepard.

"You been here all night?" Torres asked.

"I came in around 4am after Daniels was out of surgery. He's going to be ok."

"Praise the Lord." She sat down and opened the files. "Some good news."

"The bike?"

"No. The van. The bike was a dead-end. It took a while, but I went back and reviewed every hit and run for the last six weeks. A few days before Suarez was killed, a woman riding a motorcycle was struck by a vehicle and propelled into a telephone pole."

"OK. So?"

"She was mistakenly pronounced dead on the scene. She was taken to UCLA Medical. She's a Jane Doe and in a coma. No one can identify her."

"Keep going," Shepard said, getting excited.

"She was on an exotic BMW motorcycle. I think she's related to our guy. He's a motorcycle nut. This is the type of bike he'd have. She's hit. He figures out it's the 70's that did it and goes after them."

"Who is the BMW registered to?" Shepard asked.

"It's not registered at all. Weird, right?" Torres added.

"It's a big jump from the hit and run to the 70's, Torres."

"It's the best we've got."

"Let's go visit Daniels. He might even be on the same floor as Jane Doe." Shepard said, closing the laptop. "Give me 30 minutes and we'll head out."

'Copy." Torres answered, closing the folder.

Across the city, Sean was walking out of 24-Hour Fitness, freshly showered and shaved with his backpack over his shoulder and helmet in his right hand. The gym still had not figured out that he was popping in for a shower and leaving. He'd ditched the black helmet for a matte white version of the same design. He got on the bike, put the helmet on and left the lot. The Kawasaki was a sweet bike. Not as much total power as the Ducati, but it felt even more nimble and much, much faster. Sean tried to push it, but morning traffic was standing in the way. Sean took the exit off of I-10 that led to the carwash. Traffic stopped him halfway down the ramp. He pulled out onto the shoulder and made his way towards the intersection. At the bottom of the ramp was a man spinning a giant yellow sign. These guys were all over LA, selling everything from watches to car insurance. However, as Sean got closer, he noticed something very different. The sign was written in Russian Cyrillic and followed by a phone number.

The sign read: *She's still alive. 323-825-2631*

Sean skidded to a stop on the shoulder and pulled off his helmet. He knew the sign was for him. He took out one of the burner phones from his pocket and dialed the number.

"UCLA Medical Center, Intensive Care Unit. How may I help you?"

Sean lost his breath and leaned over the tank of the bike. He had the phone to his ear.

"Hello? Is anyone there?" The nurse asked.

Sean tried to catch his breath. "I'm calling for Natalia Molotov."

The nurse became very excited. "You are? Oh, that's wonderful! Until last night, she was a Jane Doe."

Sean dropped the phone on the pavement and began sobbing. He felt like he'd been punched in the gut. He was breathing heavy. "They told me she was dead. I saw her hit the pole. I saw her body." Sean said out loud in a panic. He pulled his helmet on and managed to get back on I-10 west. This time, he didn't care about the traffic and pushed the Kawasaki to its limits.

In room 4 of the ICU, Deputy Michael Daniels was recovering from a complicated surgery. Deputy Debbie Torres sat in a chair next to Daniels. Max Shepard stood at the end of the bed. All sorts of tubes were coming out of the deputy. He was stable and awake.

"Michael, did you see his face?" Shepard asked.

"No. No. The helmet's visor was down the entire time."

"What was he saying to you? When we watched the security footage, it looked like he was talking to you."

"He said he wouldn't let me die. He kept telling me I was going to be OK and wouldn't leave me until I was safe. He said it over and over. Max, those guys were going to execute me. He risked his life and getting caught to make sure I stayed alive."

Max Shepard rocked back and forth on his feet as he listened, clearly torn. Torres looked back at her boss. Shepard squeezed Daniels' foot.

"You rest. We'll be back to see you. Just get some rest," Shepard said. He motioned to Torres. She brushed Daniels' hair back from his forehead and followed her boss out of the room.

"Wow. Seeing it on video is one thing. Hearing it from him is another." Torres said.

Shepard pinched the bridge of his nose with his thumb and index finger and looked at the hospital's tile floor. "Torres, you said the Jane Doe is here right?"

"Yeah, except now she's got a name. Natalia Molotov."

"Where?" Shepard asked.

"Other side of the floor."

"Lead the way." Shepard said and followed Torres down the hall. They stopped at room 22. The door was closed, but they could hear talking inside. Shepard knocked and entered the room. A blonde woman was lying in the bed, eyes closed with various monitors hooked up to her. Three men were in the room. An older man with white hair dressed in a suit was sitting in a chair against the wall. The two other men were standing on either side of the bed. One looked to be in his 60's, was dressed nicely and about 5'11" with short white hair. The second man was tall. 6'3" at least. He had on tan pants, tan boots and a red polo shirt. The fabric of the shirt was straining against shoulders, chest and arms. He had closely cropped blonde hair.

"I'm sorry to bother you. I'm Deputy Max Shepard and this is Deputy Torres of the LA County

Sheriff's office. We'd like to ask you about Ms. Molotov."

"I'm Sergei Molotov. I'm her uncle." Sergei extended his hand as he spoke. Shepard immediately noticed the large, callused and powerful hand that dwarfed his. "This is Pavel Fetisov, Natalia's father." Pavel shook Shepard's hand. The man sitting didn't say anything.

"I'd first like say how sorry we all are about the accident. I personally would like to apologize that we don't have any leads but are working on it."

"You're with the gang task force, aren't you?" Sergei asked. "Was she a target?"

"How do you know that?" Shepard asked.

"We saw you on TV," Sergei answered, arms crossed.

"Oh, right." Shepard answered. "We don't know. Like I said, we're looking into it," Shepard explained, beginning to get nervous, which he rarely did. "Do you know why she's in LA?"

"Just visiting. She loves California." Pavel answered.

"Visiting anyone?"

"Not that I know of," Pavel said calmly.

"Do you know why she was on a motorcycle?"

"She loves bikes. We're trying to figure out where she got the bike," Sergei added.

"So are we." Shepard looked both Sergei and Pavel in the eyes for a moment. "Well, thank you. Sorry to have bothered you. We are all praying she makes a full recovery. Is there a way to get in contact with you?"

"Here's my card," Pavel said, fishing a business card out of his jacket pocket and handing it to Shepard.

"Thank you." Shepard replied, gesturing with the business card. He and Torres left and went down the hall. Shepard was walking very fast.

"Max! Max! Stop!" Torres shouted. Shepard stopped in front of the elevators. "What's going on? I've never seen you act like that."

"Did you see who was in that room? Hmmm?" Shepard said, looking down the hallway as he spoke.

"Yeah."

"I don't think you did. The guy sitting in the chair. The one who didn't speak? That was David O'Connor, the former director of the CIA."

"Shit."

"The big guy? I'm guessing he's some sort of operator."

"What do you mean?"

"He's probably former special forces. Based on his surname, I'd bet he was Spetsnaz. The other guy too."

"How do you know that?" Torres said, pushing the button for the elevator.

"Look, I saw those SF guys in Iraq. I'll never forget the eyes some of them had. Sergei? That guy has them. We don't want to tangle with him. Guys like him operate in another world."

Outside, Sean pulled the bike into the medical center's parking lot and got off and started walking to the hospital. He noticed several LA County Sheriff's Department vehicles in the lot. He didn't care.

Back in the hospital, Torres glared at her boss. They stepped into the elevator. The doors closed. Torres slapped his face. "Get a grip! I don't give a shit if that's the CIA director or not. We've got a job to do. We're both upset about Daniels. Let's figure this thing out."

Shepard looked at Torres. "You're right. Daniels' shooting got to me. It doesn't matter who was in that room. There's more."

"What else?" Torres asked

"The girl lying in the bed is a special individual. If the CIA director is here, she's special."

"You think that guy Sergei is behind this?"

Shepard shook his head. "No. I'm certain he's capable, however. No, our guy makes the two back in that room look like boy scouts. If he's connected with the CIA, we might never see him again and we can forget about arresting him." The doors opened and the two deputies walked across the lobby. Coming the opposite way, down the walkway outside was a man dressed in jeans and a t-shirt with a backpack on. He was a couple inches taller than Shepard. Shepard held the door open for him.

"Thanks buddy," Sean said, passing the deputies, entering the hospital and heading straight for the elevator bank.

"Have they located Roberto Flores yet? He knows he has a target on his back." Torres asked. Shepard didn't answer. He stopped walking.

"Did you see that guy?" Shepard asked, looking back at the hospital entrance.

"No. Why?"

"His voice. It sounds familiar. I know I've seen him."

"Max, get some sleep. You're exhausted."

"You're right. I'll go home and get some sleep." Shepard said, faking a smile. They walked into the parking garage toward their vehicles. As they passed Sean's lime green bike, Torres whistled.

"Now, that's nice bike!" she said, examining the bike. "No plate. I'm too tired to write a ticket." Shepard made a face at her, then stopped dead in his tracks.

"Look at that! He's here!" Shepard said, walking over to the Kawasaki and kneeling down to look it over.

"That's not a Ducati, Max," Torres said, hands on her hips.

"No. He's too careful. He wouldn't ride it again. But a guy that has a bike like the Ducati probably has another one. You said it yourself!" Shepard said, spotting a plaque on the gas tank. "Number 427 out of 500. This is a rare bike, Torres. I'm telling you. He's here and if I was a betting man, I'd wager he walked right past us on the way into the parking lot."

"The guy with the backpack? He looked kind of clueless."

Shepard was unlocking his truck and slapping a clip into his M4. "Yeah that guy and he's not clueless. We're going to wait right here. This whole thing could go sideways fast with Sergei in the room with our guy. Plus, we have no idea who the CIA director has with him.

"So, you think he's heading up to Molotov's room? He's CIA?"

"Yeah. If he's not CIA, he's some sort of a CIA asset and a dangerous one. Get your weapon. We're waiting for him right here."

Sean got off the elevator and looked around. He was more nervous than he'd ever been in his life. A nurse noticed that he looked lost.

"Can I help you?"

Sean was looking up and down the hall. He stammered slightly. "Molotov."

"Oh! Yes! She's in 22. We're so glad her family is here." the nurse said.

"Her family?"

"Yes, they came in last night."

"22?"

"Yes, right down there." The nurse said, pointing down the hall. Sean took off in a jog, slowing when he approached the room. He opened the door and pulled back the curtain. He took off the backpack and let it drop to the ground. Nat was motionless on the hospital bed. Her legs and one of her arms were broken. Her head was bandaged. Sergei, Pavel and David O'Connor stood up when he entered. Sean began welling up with tears. He stood next to her bed, took her hand and fell to a knee. O'Connor kicked the backpack over to Sergei, who picked it up and removed Sean's Glock and three clips. Sean didn't notice.

"I'm so, so sorry. I didn't know. I didn't know you were here. They told me you died." Sean burst into tears and pressed his head into the sheets on the bed, clutching Nat's hand. Pavel put his hand on Sean's shoulder.

"Sean. Sean. Come here," Pavel said, helping Sean to his feet and wrapping his arms around him.

"I'm sorry Pavel. I'm sorry. I wasn't there."

"Sean, I'm glad you're here now. It's not your fault," Pavel assured Sean.

Sergei stood a few feet away with his arms crossed with a heart broken look on his face. When Pavel released Sean, Sergei took him by the arm and hugged him as well. "Sean, I'm sorry. Sorry this has happened. We're here for you and for Natalia."

David O'Connor was also moved. The combination of seeing Sergei a man he'd known for 40 years and Sean, someone he felt responsible for in such emotional distress weighed on him. He patted Sean on the shoulder in the most reassuring and comforting way he could. Sean tried to compose himself.

"What did they say?" Sean asked.

"It's not good. She was mistakenly pronounced dead on the scene, and she's been barely hanging on since. She's in a medically induced coma. I'm meeting with the doctors in the morning."

Sean was shaking his head with his hands on his hips. He was having trouble keeping it together. "Do you mind if I'm here in the morning?"

"I'd like for you to be. She'd want you to be," Pavel said.

No one in the room asked about the war Sean was conducting against one of LA's worst street gangs.

"I have a few things to take care of and I'll be back to sit with her," Sean said, picking up his backpack, not noticing the reduction in weight of the bag.

The three men watched him leave and walk down the hall.

"Sergei, you need to go stop him. Two things are about to happen. He's going to go straight to that carwash to end this or there are 20 LA County Sheriff's deputies in the lobby waiting for him with their guns drawn." O'Connor said.

"I don't know how successful I'll be." Sergei said.

"I just need him to stay here. Stall him." O'Connor added. Sergei left the room.

Sean got off the elevator, left the hospital and entered the parking garage. He rounded a corner to find two LA County deputies pointing M4s at him.

"ON THE GROUND NOW!" Max Shepard screamed at Sean. Sean put his hands up but didn't go to the ground.

"What's going on? I'm just visiting my friend. You have the wrong guy," Sean said, slowly circling, trying to put something between him and the deputies. Sean started to slide off his backpack.

"DON'T MAKE ME SHOOT YOU!"

"I'm taking off my pack. It's got my license in it," Sean said calmly, dropping the pack and sliding it over. The deputies didn't move.

"ON THE GROUND!" Shepard repeated. As he screamed, Sergei came around the corner and saw what was going on.

"Easy. Easy." Sergei said, placing his hands above his head. Shepard saw this as the worst possible scenario. He believed the two most dangerous men in LA were right in front of him.

"BOTH OF YOU ON THE GROUND!"

"Do it," Sergei said to Sean. Sean complied and went to his knees as did Sergei.

"Cover me," Shepard said to Torres.

# No Shortcut Home

"I've got you."

Sergei looked at Sean and didn't like what he saw. Sean clearly was preparing to take down Shepard.

"Sean, don't. Trust me. We will work this out." Sergei said to Sean. Sean glared at him with eyes Sergei never wanted to see again. "Trust me," Sergei repeated.

Shepard walked behind Sean and pushed him to the ground and slapped cuffs on his wrists. "Now you. I don't know if you're involved in this or not." He pulled Sergei's arms behind his back and cuffed him as he spoke. Shepard placed both of them with their backs against the concrete wall of the parking garage. He studied Sean and after a moment began waving his finger.

"I've got it. I know where I know you. Roscoe's. You were leaving and held the door for us. You remember?"

Sean didn't answer.

"Funny thing about Roscoe's, it gives you the perfect place to watch Roberto Flores and his crew." He kicked Sean's boot. "I've got you!"

Sean looked Shepard up and down but didn't respond.

In East Los Angeles two black vans led by a black motorcycle sped down East 4$^{th}$ Street weaving in and out of traffic. They passed Roscoe's Chicken and Waffles and stopped in front of the 70's carwash. The rider of the motorcycle got off the bike, pulled the pin on the grenade in his hand and threw it into the tunnel of the carwash. The explosion rocked the building. Six men with AK47s burst out of the vans. Roberto Flores came around the side of the building firing a pistol. The six men opened fire, cutting him down. Three more 70's ran out of the carwash office. They were killed instantly by rounds from the AK47s. One of the men from the van tossed the man on the motorcycle a can of red spray paint. He proceeded to tag the pavement with a Triad symbol. The van sped away from the scene, followed by a man on a black Ducati Panigale VR4.

Back at the UCLA Medical Center, David O'Connor was paged. He left Nat's room and picked up a phone.

"David, it's been handled," said a heavily accented Chinese voice.

"Thank you, old friend. I owe you one," O'Connor responded.

"After meeting him in Ottawa, I see why you like him."

"Let's have dinner soon." O'Connor said.

"Yes, soon. Bring your man along. I think I'd enjoy speaking with him," The man said and hung up.

In the parking garage, Sean had already slipped his cuffs. He watched the deputies on the radio.

"Sean, trust me. You have to trust me. Don't do anything."

Sean shot Sergei another nasty look and then turned his attention back to the deputies. His hands were free, but he kept them behind his back. Max Shepard was standing next to his truck on the radio. He was clearly agitated. He threw the radio into the truck and walked over to Sean and Sergei. He was unarmed.

"Get up."

Sergei and Sean got to their feet.

"Turn around." Shepard removed Sergei's cuffs.

"Mine fell off," Sean said, holding the cuffs in his hand. Sergei turned and stared at Sean.

"They just 'fell' off?" Shepard said and got eye to eye with Sean. Sean dropped the cuffs into his hand. "Look, I know it was you. The Triads were never involved. Today was bullshit."

"I don't know what you mean," Sean responded. Shepard turned and threw the handcuffs off the side of his truck, leaving a good-sized dent. Torres made a hand gesture telling him to calm down. She picked up the cuffs and tossed them in the truck.

Sergei stood next to Sean and whispered in Russian. "I see you have the same effect on him as you do me."

"Thank you," Sean answered back in Russian.

Shepard walked over to the Kawasaki and pointed at the back of the bike. "Get a fucking plate on this thing before I impound it."

"Yes sir," Sean answered. Shepard got in his truck, slammed the door and left the parking lot followed by Torres in her car.

Sergei put his hand on Sean's back. "I need to talk to you." Sean followed Sergei out of the garage. He pointed at a bench under a tree in front of the hospital. "Sit." Sergei sat next to him. "I just want you to listen."

"Ok." Sean answered, turning towards Sergei. He could tell Sergei was nervous, which was very uncharacteristic.

"Sean, I'm not going to ask you about what's been going on."

"Thank you."

"Just listen, please. I know you have a difficult time trusting me and trusting Ana and for good reason. We want a second chance and want you in our lives."

Sean leaned forward, still emotional from seeing Nat and now he was doubly upset.

Sergei continued, "I know you want to be closer to Michelle, and I think you need us. You need to be around people that care about you." He put his hand on Sean's back. "Sean, we do care about you."

Sean was not expecting this at all. "I'd like that."

"And another thing, I'm staying out of whatever is going on between you and Ana. That's between you two. I want you to know I'm always in your corner. Always."

"That means a lot. Thank you, Sergei," Sean said.

"Two other things."

"Yeah."

"David wants you to travel to D.C. He wants to debrief with you, members of the CIA and NSA."

"I thought he was fired?" Sean asked.

"He's an advisor. Guys like David are never really out, Sean. As you saw, he clearly has a good relationship with the Chinese."

"Right."

"He also wants you to talk to someone about what's going on in your head."

"A shrink?"

"I wouldn't think of it that way, but yes, I suppose 'shrink' is accurate. A lot of our best operators talk to this doctor. In our business, we see some terrible things and need to talk about it."

"And I have more baggage than anyone," Sean said, slightly embarrassed.

"Sean, some terrible things have happened to you. We all want you to come out of it stronger and healthier and . . . ."

"Normal?"

Sergei laughed, "I don't think you'll ever be normal."

"Funny."

"Seriously, we want to help you cope with what's happened to you. That's all."

"I'll go. Don't worry."

"I knew you'd agree. Pavel wants you to stay with him when you're in D.C."

"You sure?"

"Sean, we all love you. What happened to Natalia was not your fault. No one thinks that it was your fault. You need to realize that."

Sean wiped a tear from his face.

"The second thing I need to tell you is that Natalia is not going to make it. She's been on life support and the doctors are telling us that she's now brain dead."

Sean sobbed. Sergei put his hand on his back.

"Pavel is going to have to make a horrible decision in the next 12 hours."

"I'll be there for him – and Nat." Sean said, sobbing as he spoke. "I don't know how, but I will."

"I'll be there with you both. She's going to a better place."

"Yeah."

They both sat in silence for several moments before Sergei tried to change the subject.

"So, a HALO jump? I didn't know you were qualified?"

"I am now," Sean said, trying to smile. "And onto the roof of a building . . . .and at night." Sean stood as he was speaking. He looked at Sergei still sitting on the bench.

"I'd love to make a jump like that," Sergei said.

"I'm sorry. There's a weight limit. You might have to go on a diet." Sean laughed knowing Sergei had not been out of shape any day of his life.

"You calling me fat?" Sergei said, getting to his feet.

"No. No. That would be mean."

"Don't make me regret the second chance talk. Let's go back upstairs." They entered the hospital, got off the elevator and headed towards room 22. Halfway down the hall, Sean saw the name "Daniels" on the door of room. He stopped.

"Sergei, I'll be there in a minute."

Sergei looked at the name on the door and knew it was the deputy Sean had risked his life saving. "Sean, I don't know if that's a good idea. In fact, it's stupid."

"Thank you for that. I'll be right there." Sergei shook his head and continued down the hall. Sean knocked on deputy Daniels' door.

"Hello?" Sean said, opening the door.

"Yes?" Daniels answered.

"Ok to come in?"

"Yes." Sean entered the room. "I'm sorry, do I know you?" Daniels asked. "I'm pretty doped up right now. If I am a little fuzzy, I apologize."

Sean looked at the various wires and tubes attached to the deputy. Periodically, a machine beeped. He stood at the end of the bed. "No, you don't know me."

"Are you ok sir?" Daniels asked, now scrutinizing Sean.

"My friend is down the hall. She not going to make it."

"I'm sorry to hear that. Losing someone is so hard," Daniels answered. Sean nodded.

"I saw other deputies here earlier. I just wanted to check on you and tell you I hope you get better. You guys have a tough and sometimes thankless job. Thank you for what you do and I'm sorry you're here," Sean said.

"Thank you for saying that. I'm actually getting moved out of here today. That's good news."

"That is great news," Sean said, forcing a smile. "I'm going back down the hall. Take care of yourself. Ok buddy?" he said, tapping the end of the bed with his hand and turning to leave.

The word "buddy" bounced around in Deputy Daniel's head for a second or two. "Hey!"

Sean turned around. "Yeah."

"I think I know you."

Sean made a face. "I don't think so. I'm not from around here."

"You saved my life. I wouldn't be here if it wasn't for you," Daniels said.

"Sorry. Not me, but I'm glad you're ok."

"You risked everything to save me and then waited for the EMTs and didn't leave until you knew I had help. I'll never forget your voice."

"Not me buddy. Sorry." Sean pointed at the IV and wiggled his finger. "Might be the stuff they're filling you with."

"It's not. I'll never forget you. Thank you."

"Again, not me." Sean opened the door and started to leave and then stuck his head back in. "Moving forward, don't take your vest off until you get home."

"Wait!" Daniels shouted at Sean.

Sean shut the door and walked down the hall to room #22. He stood outside the door for a split second, took a deep breath, quietly opened the door and closed it behind him.

##END##

**Sean will return later in 2020**

Made in the USA
Columbia, SC
30 March 2020